DARK MYSTERY

Dark Mystery

A Patrick Dawlish Mystery

John Creasey *writing as* Gordon Ashe

OPEN ROAD

INTEGRATED MEDIA
NEW YORK

ISBN: 978-1-5040-9810-6

This edition published in 2024 by Open Road Integrated Media, Inc.
180 Maiden Lane
New York, NY 10038
www.openroadmedia.com

DARK MYSTERY

CHAPTER ONE

FREDDIE

The door of the club-house opened and a large young man put his head into the room.

'Anyone seen Freddie?' he demanded in a deep voice.

'Not since lunch,' answered a middle-aged man sitting at the writing-desk. 'Confound you, either come in or stay out!' He grabbed at several sheets of paper which rose from the table as a gust of wind swept in. 'There's no peace in this place these days, I don't know what you young fellows are coming to. You've no—'

The young man dropped on one knee. 'My dear Speck, a thousand apologies.' He picked up a sheet of paper half-covered with writing, and rubbed off a speck of dust. 'As good as new—'

'Give that to me!' The man called Speck snatched at it.

The other stared at him, perplexed, then shrugged good-humouredly. 'You haven't seen Freddie, have you?'

'No,' declared the other shortly. 'I have not seen Appleyard since lunch.' He placed his hand on the half-written letter.

The young man turned away and approached the bar. It was three o'clock in the afternoon and the elderly attendant, called at the Sola Tennis Club a stewardess, was deep in a book propped up on a whisky glass.

'Bunny,' said the young man, mildly, 'how about half-a-pint?'

The stewardess, her eyes still on her book, said mechanically: 'You know we can't do anything like that, Mr. Gratton, I don't know how many times I have to tell you. Have a nice ginger beer.'

Gratton shuddered.

'Do you wish to *kill* me?' he asked plaintively. 'By the way, have you seen Mr. Appleyard?'

'Mr. *who*? Oh, Freddie. No I haven't. Not since lunch that is.' She sniffed. 'Told me that he was going to play you this afternoon at half-past two.'

'That was the original idea,' agreed Gratton.

'It wouldn't surprise me if he'd dozed off in one of the armchairs. Can't do a young man any good to be hanging around a dull old place like this half the day. Mark my words, that's where you'll find him, for sure,' declared Bunny, her gaze straying back to her book.

Gratton strolled across the large room towards a door in the corner marked '*Card Room*'. The *Sola* was a large club, with twenty hard and a dozen grass courts. In the club room itself, cane chairs lined the walls and there were four writing-desks; why Speck chose the draughty one near the door Gratton could not imagine, unless it was to be purposefully uncomfortable and blame someone else for it.

No one glanced up as Gratton looked through once again to make sure that Freddie was not tucked away in some dark corner. No, he was not there. Gratton went through another doorway marked '*Men's Dressing Rooms*' and walked along a narrow passage past the baths and showers.

The main dressing-room was at the far end, a large chamber with locker-seats round the walls. No one was inside, but on a peg in the corner hung a dark grey lounge suit, and on the floor stood a pair of black shoes with socks tucked neatly into them. So Freddie had changed.

'Where *has* the beggar got to?' asked Gratton aloud. He lit a cigarette rather aimlessly. Pity he was late. The wind was getting up, and it would probably be almost impossible to play in an hour's time.

This Spring holiday was proving a wash-out.

Toby Gratton, junior partner in a small firm of suburban solicitors, would have preferred to take it later in the year, but so, he discovered grimly, had his senior partners.

Where was the chap?

Curious business altogether. If he'd gone out on to the courts, surely one of the couples in the club-room would have noticed him. And there was only the one door from the dressing-room.

The windows were all closed.

'Not that he would have gone out of a window,' Gratton mused aloud.

A curious sound cut across his thoughts.

He stared about him. Nothing moved. Yet there was no doubt about the sound which had come from somewhere in the dressing-room. The lid of a locker, not properly fastened, might have slipped down.

There it was again. He stood quite still, listening. The noise came from the far corner, between two of the windows.

The lid of a locker moved up an inch, then dropped with a hollow thud—the same sound that he had heard before. Mystified, he strode towards it.

He couldn't make head or tail of it. Was this Freddie's idea of a joke? And if so, how could he have locked himself in? Gratton tried the padlock; it was securely fastened and he hadn't a key— Bunny had a master-key.

'Is that you, Freddie?' he called anxiously.

The lid rose: *bump!*

'Say something!' snapped Gratton.

Bump!

'This is crazy,' said Gratton. 'All right, I'll be back in a moment,' he promised, and turned and hurried towards the club-room. The best thing to do was to ask Bunny for the master-key, pretending he'd left his own behind; she wouldn't refuse the request of a member of the committee. He entered the club-room, and Speck, who was looking towards the door, turned back to his writing. Bunny was crouching closely over her book.

'Let me have the master-key, Bunny, I've left mine at home.'

She groped under the bar, found, and handed him the key, her mind bemused with the lurid romance she had been reading.

Gratton hurried back to the dressing-room. He pushed the key into the padlock, turned it, and pulled up the lid.

To his astonishment, all he saw was a crumpled bath towel!

Fantastic! He bent down and pushed his hands into the locker; he could feel Freddie's body beneath it. What on earth—

It wasn't easy to lift the man out of the locker, but he managed it slowly. Freddie—it could only be Freddie—was doubled up, legs nearly touching his chin. The towel was tied round at each end, with string, and the knot was too secure to be unpicked easily. Gratton took out a penknife and cut the string.

If this were a practical joke—

He pulled the towel aside; the first thing he saw was a tumbled mass of black hair.

This was a girl!

CHAPTER TWO

THE DISTRESSED YOUNG LADY

She was breathing with difficulty, because of a scarf tied round her mouth, gagging her. Gratton fumbled with the knot of the scarf, prising it loose.

'The foul brutes!' he exclaimed.

The scarf had bitten into the girl's cheeks, making the corners of her mouth white and ridged. She gasped for breath, keeping her mouth wide open.

'All right,' said Gratton in a strangled voice, 'I'll look after you.' He put her down gently, cutting the cords which bound her. She flinched as they fell away.

'Take it easy,' he urged, 'you'll be all right.' But it was infuriating to be so helpless; he knew how she felt; cramp was torturing her, and the hard wood of the locker wasn't exactly a feather bed. He picked the girl up again and held her in his arms.

'Take it easy,' he repeated mechanically. Of course the thing to do was to carry her into the club-room, Bunny could take her into the women's dressing-room and look after her; there would certainly be more comfort there. But the thought of the avid curiosity and inevitable publicity which this course would bring down on the girl, deterred him.

'Any better?' he asked, after a few minutes. She nodded. He went on: 'I'm going to lay you on the lockers, you're too cramped up here.'

This time she was able to stretch out her legs a little although she still kept her knees bent. He took off his coat to make a pillow.

'Now just move about gently,' he said, 'and I'll get you a drink.'

As he hurried to the wash-room, he tried in vain to make some sense out of the situation. To search for Freddie and find this girl—how fantastic! There was no other word that would describe it. How had she got into the dressing-room? Who had put her there?

Gratton hurried across with the glass of water, helped her to sit up, and held the glass to her lips. She drank slowly at first, letting the water fill her mouth before swallowing it. The ridges made by the scarf cut, sharp and dead white, across her cheeks.

'Thank you,' she muttered.

'Splendid!' said Gratton. 'But I shouldn't try to talk too much yet. I think I'd better help you along to the main room, the stewardess—'

'No. No—'

She seemed very anxious to stay where she was, and Gratton had no wish to cause a sensation in the club-room. Soon she would be able to talk more freely, and in a few minutes he would ask for explanations. He was uneasy, in case Freddie was responsible for her plight; he was a friend of Freddie. Bunny and Old Speck would almost certainly connect the disappearance of Freddie with the remarkable misadventure of the girl. There was, too, a smaller, more nagging worry. If anyone came to the room he would be caught breaking one of the strictest rules of the club; no mixing in the dressing-rooms. But the wind was howling fiercely, and anyone who had considered tennis that day would surely have given it up.

He kept some vaseline in his locker, fetched it, smeared a little over his fingers and began to massage the girl's cheeks. All the time he worked, she continued to move her arms and legs cautiously. Once or twice she flinched or grimaced at a spasm of pain, but her colour became more natural and her eyes much clearer.

She was quite young—in the early twenties, he imagined—attractive in a rather boyish way; her hair, long and dark, was really lovely.

After a while, she struggled feebly to get up.

He helped her from the locker. She was unsteady when she first rose to her feet, and he had to keep his arms round her. Then she insisted on trying to walk alone. Swaying a little she managed to reach the locker again without much difficulty. She smiled up at him.

'You'll be all right soon,' said Gratton. He added, cautiously: 'What happened?'

She said simply: 'A fat man tied me up.'

'Fat, eh?' echoed Gratton, with a sigh of relief; no one in their senses could call Freddie fat.

'I see,' said Gratton. 'Er—I don't want to appear unduly curious, but I am, you know. Curious, I mean.'

'Of course you are,' she said. 'But I'd rather tell you everything at one go. Just now, I'm a bit—shaky.'

'Hardly surprising,' commented Gratton. 'There's no hurry at all. On the other hand, we ought to find out more about it. You might have been suffocated.'

He realised as he spoke, that this girl had nearly been murdered. The realisation did something to his stomach; he felt queasy.

'We'll find out,' said the girl, 'but now I'm going to try to walk again. I'll manage on my own this time,' she added, when he started to help her.

He put a finger to his lips.

Two or three people were coming towards the club-house from the main gates; he could hear them talking, and did not want them to hear the girl's voice. They passed the window, one very tall, powerful-looking fellow with a broken nose, whom Gratton had never seen before, and a tall, graceful woman, as well as young Plomley, a new member. They disappeared.

'Sorry,' said Gratton. 'The responsibility of a committee man weighs heavily on me. Years ago, I thought it great fun to smuggle a girl in here. Now I have to put away childish amusements. Er—what I mean to say—' He paused, feeling a little sheepish. 'The truth is, we ought to go into the club-room, you're not looking so bad now. Can you face it?'

'Yes, of course,' said the girl. 'If I could have another glass of water first, I'd be grateful.'

He liked her spirit. Walking towards the wash-room, he reflected soberly that it was undoubtedly true that she had nearly been murdered. How long could a girl—or anyone—remain gagged like that and confined in a small, almost airless locker? Shuddering thought, that the owner of that locker might have opened it one day and found a corpse.

Gratton filled the glass and hurried back to the dressing-room. As he did so, he heard a car start up in the parking place outside.

He opened the door.

'Just what the doctor ordered,' he said cheerfully, 'pure, unadulterated and—'

He broke off in astonishment, for the room was empty. An open window banged aimlessly.

CHAPTER THREE

A MAN NAMED DAWLISH

One swift glance round the room satisfied Gratton that the girl had gone, and he crossed hurriedly to the window and leaned out.

The large man who had come with Plomley sprinted past him towards the gate. Gratton caught a glimpse of keen blue eyes; they seemed to look through him and then dismiss him as of no account. The car, which was out of sight, turned into the main road; the sound of changing gears was unmistakable.

Gratton felt speechless.

He drew his head back and sat heavily on a locker. No one would believe what had happened; it seemed dreamlike even to him, but—the girl *had* been inside the locker, he *had* untied the cords that bound her, she *had* asked for a glass of water.

He felt suddenly angry.

She had made sure she could walk freely before letting him go for the drink, and had intended to get away. Now he understood why she had been anxious not to go into the club-room. She had planned to make a fool of him. Confound the little brat!

A gust of wind slammed against the window, and in the ensuing lull he heard another car starting up. He jumped to his feet. He could not mistake the sound of that engine; it was his own. A little splutter and cough, three pulls at the self-starter, and a peculiarly piercing squeak as the hand-brake was eased off.

He pushed the window open, climbed out, and dropped lightly to the asphalt path. Next moment, he saw his little green two-seater sports car moving towards the open gates. He put on a burst of speed and shouted:

'Stop, you! Stop!'

The driver was Plomley's guest.

Gratton couldn't tell whether the man heard his shout; but he took not the slightest notice of him. A woman crossed the roadway leading into the club, however, and the driver was forced to stop. Gratton grabbed the door.

'*Stop!*' he roared.

The large man gave him another searching glance.

'Hop in,' he said.

He shot out his left arm, gripping Gratton's wrist as he swung the car out of the club gateway. But for the grip, Gratton would have fallen. Undoubtedly, if he wanted to see that his car was safe, he must not leave it. The driver had the grace to slow down a little, and Gratton climbed in.

'Now look here—'

'Explanations later,' said the large man. 'Apologies now, if you like, and I'll pay for any damage. Mind if I concentrate on driving?'

Gratton sat fuming by his side.

A long ribbon of road stretched ahead of them, with fields on either side. The engine wasn't going too well. Gratton knew its peculiarities; he was extremely fond of the little car. It could do fifty-five comfortably and sixty-five at a stretch, but any more would ruin the ancient engine. He glanced at the speedometer, and exclaimed aloud.

'Now look here—' he began, angrily.

'You can tell me all about it later,' said the big man, 'and I'll promise not to answer back! Meanwhile you might keep an eye on that Bentley in front. It's going between the trees and might turn right or left.'

'Damn the Bentley!'

'Hold hard,' protested the large man, 'it's mine.'

'Yours!' gasped Gratton.

'And whether it's stolen or whether it's borrowed I wouldn't like to say,' said the driver. 'I wish—'

A gust of wind took the words out of his mouth. The only sensible thing to do, decided Gratton, was to wait until this absurd chase was over. There might be some excuse for the man's action.

Had the *girl* taken the Bentley?

Suddenly the leading car broke from the avenue of trees. A vivid splash of sunlight shone on it, but Gratton could not see the driver.

'What can it do?' he asked suddenly.

'I've touched a hundred and twenty. I hope she doesn't.'

'She?'

'Lightfingered Lucy,' said the big man with a grin. 'Hold tight at this corner.'

Gratton held on grimly as the car swung right. He had discovered one thing; this man was a driver in a thousand, and it would take a great deal to cause an accident; on the other hand the fellow was new to this car and didn't know the road, and the car couldn't be relied on at such a speed.

'Look out!' he screamed.

There was a left-hand turn just beyond the corner and as they drew near it, Gratton saw a branch lying across the road. It left no room for the car to pass, and at this speed it was impossible to stop.

The driver had the sense not to jam on the brakes, had he done so they would have overturned; but—could they slow down in time? They *were* slowing down, but the branch was only a few yards ahead.

The front wheels bumped over the obstruction, the car shuddered and came to a stop. Gratton leaned back in his seat, wiping the sweat from his forehead, but the driver needed no such respite. He jumped out.

'Hop out a minute, will you? I think I can manage it if you'll pull the tree away.' Without another word he went to the back of the car, bent down and gripped the underside of the carriage, and raised it several inches from the ground. It was a feat of strength which took Gratton's breath away.

The branch was an old one; twigs broke from it as he pulled it free; a few dead leaves danced about in the wind. As soon as it was clear the big man lowered the car.

'We're probably too late,' he remarked, 'but I think we ought to have another try. Isn't there a hill a couple of miles along?'

Gratton nodded as he climbed back.

A tradesman's van and a lorry passed them before they reached the top of the hill. From there they had a panoramic view of broken country. A few cars moved along this road and another crossed it two miles away. Gratton couldn't be sure whether the Bentley was one of them, but the driver seemed sure enough.

'She's gone,' he said. 'Nice work, wasn't it?'

'That's one way of looking at it,' said Gratton.

'Oh, let's be fair. She nobbled the car, showed me a clean pair of tyre tracks, and fixed the tree. She didn't do that on her own, of course, that's interesting—the most interesting thing about it.'

'Are you mad?' demanded Gratton. 'Fixed what tree?'

The big man chuckled.

'That branch didn't fall from one of the nearby trees. It was poplar. The trees where we came across it are beech. It must have been put there. Careful job, too, it stretched from side to side. Not a friendly act, when you come to think of it, we might have broken our necks. Interesting point—would anyone have suspected murder?'

'Mur—' Gratton began, and stopped. This was the second time within an hour he had contemplated the act of murder. An attempt to murder the girl and an attempt to crash the car? But he had only this man's opinion about that attempt, it might not be true.

'Nice game you've got mixed up in,' murmured the driver. 'I suppose we'd better turn back.'

'I suppose you're sure the Bentley's not in sight,' said Gratton, shielding his eyes against the wind.

'Pretty sure. I hope they don't wreck that bus, I was getting fond of her. As you're fond of this one, I suppose,' he added, reversing skilfully. 'Had her long?'

'Eleven years,' confessed Gratton.

'And still game,' remarked the big man, 'these were always little beauties and you picked a good year.'

They went along in silence for a couple of miles, until they came to the avenue of trees. The branch of the poplar was still placed neatly at the side of the road, and the big man pulled up and got out to examine it more closely. After a few seconds he found a gap in the hedge and squeezed through. Gratton stood watching him. But for his broken nose the big fellow would have been remarkably handsome; he had a square chin with a cleft and a good brow. He was examining the ground on the other side of the hedge, and, unable to restrain his curiosity, Gratton pushed through and joined him.

'Lost something?'

'Looking for something, which isn't quite the same thing,' said the big fellow absently. 'Two men, I'd say. One large, the other smallish—shoes or boots size ten and eight respectively.' He pointed to some impressions in the damp ground close to the hedge, then offered cigarettes from a large gold case. Gratton took a cigarette without speaking, and followed his companion back to the car.

'Care to drive?' asked the big man.

Gratton laughed.

'As you've started the job you may as well finish it,' he said. 'Care to answer a few questions?'

The stranger looked at Gratton, and there was no hint of levity in his expression.

'Right! This may be as good a time as any. Name, Dawlish. Business, fruit-farming, and side-lines. Pet aversion—' he paused, 'the police.'

After a lengthy silence, Gratton said:

'It rather looks as if you'll have to meet your pet aversion, doesn't it?'

'Why?'

'I thought you wanted your car back.'

'Not so badly as all that,' said Dawlish. He began to smile, and there was a friendly gleam in his eyes. 'I'd much rather work this out for myself. I'm sorry you caught up with me, I would have returned the car and made full amends and all would have ended happily. How well do you know Plomley?'

'Only slightly,' said Gratton, taken aback by the sudden change of subject.

'Pity,' said Dawlish. 'You think he's a swollen-headed young ass who wants kicking, don't you?'

'Kicking is one word for it,' said Gratton.

'Pity,' repeated Dawlish. 'Plomley's all right, but he takes some knowing. He would recommend me as being fairly reliable, but I'll have to convince you of that some other way. Well, ask on. What do you want to know?'

Until that moment questions had been jostling one another in Gratton's mind; now he couldn't think of one.

'Oh, I hardly know where to start,' he said irritably, 'let's get back. It's too cold here.' When Dawlish let in the clutch again, he added ruefully: 'Why the devil you don't rush to the nearest telephone to report that your car's been stolen, I don't know!'

'Call it a private war,' said Dawlish, as the car moved off. 'You know, Gratton, if you were wise you'd forget this ever happened. You'd be much better off in the end.'

'Nonsense!' snapped Gratton. 'I'm going to know the answers.'

'Then you're a cleverer man than I,' said Dawlish drily. 'I've been looking for them for weeks, and I don't seem any nearer knowing them. A pretty girl in some distress who bites the hand that feeds her, and—'

'*What* did you say?' exclaimed Gratton.

Dawlish looked at him. 'What's on your mind? You haven't met this girl before, have you?'

'Met her?—oh, I can't make head or tail of it,' exclaimed Gratton, 'from the time that Freddie let me down, it's been a nightmare. And you're part of it,' he declared sourly.

'Freddie?' echoed Dawlish in a curiously quiet voice. 'Not, by any chance, Freddie Appleyard?'

'So you know him?'

'We're acquainted,' said Dawlish. 'How did he let you down?'

'We were due to play tennis and he didn't turn up. It's queer, because he changed and was at the club about two o'clock, but—Steady, you fool!' for the car had suddenly shot forward. 'Do you want to break our necks?'

'No,' said Dawlish, 'but I'd like to save Freddie's.'

CHAPTER FOUR

A STORY FROM DAWLISH

Freddie had not returned when they reached the club-house, although twenty or thirty people were having tea—including Plomley and the graceful woman. Dawlish stayed at their table just long enough to make sure that Freddie hadn't turned up, then said he'd be back in a few minutes, and hurried off.

'Who *is* that fellow?' demanded Gratton irritably. 'He behaves like a madman. What's he gone shooting off for now? He nearly broke my neck, he's ruined my car, and—'

'I'm so sorry,' said the woman, 'I'm afraid he's rather like that.'

'You ought to know,' said Plomley, grinning. 'Sit down, Gratton, and have some tea. This is Mrs. Dawlish—the giant's wife, who has far more to put up with than you.'

'Patronising oaf,' thought Gratton, but he forced a rather sheepish smile. 'Your husband's a bit overpowering, isn't he?'

Mrs. Dawlish laughed. 'He didn't *actually* break your neck, did he?'

'Good deed deferred,' grinned Plomley.

Gratton looked at him sourly.

'You'd better have some fresh tea,' said Mrs. Dawlish,

comfortably. 'Call a waitress, Dick. Pat's sure to be hungry, he had hardly anything for lunch. Here he is,' she added.

Dawlish strolled across the room, dropped into a chair, beamed at his wife, and helped himself to a cake.

'I am a large man with a large appetite,' he announced gravely, to a passing waitress, 'and I know you'll do the best you can for me.'

'Y-y-y-yes, sir!'

'Ask Bunny if there's a plate of cold meat,' said Plomley.

'Y-y-yes, sir.'

'And everything that goes with it,' added Plomley. He was popular with the staff, and the girl would undoubtedly do her best.

Dawlish looked round at the various tea drinkers. 'We're fairly secluded here,' he remarked, 'not a bad spot to talk, after all. I am about to take Gratton into our confidence,' he paused, as if for comment; none was made. 'The girl who took my car, Gratton, is an extremely rich young woman. And I really mean rich. She's also wayward, and mixes with some pretty queer people. She got herself into a jam with an unpleasant young man, and asked me to lend a hand. Which I did—or tried to do. Following me so far?'

Gratton said slowly: 'Yes, so far.'

'For "rich", read "millionairess",' murmured Plomley.

'In her own right,' contributed Mrs. Dawlish.

'And what is known as alone in the world,' went on Dawlish. 'That is, she has no close relatives and few, if any, trustworthy friends. A lonely thing, wealth. The sycophants and parasites hover around and too many folk keep their distance because it may be thought that they're also out for pickings. I think that about sums up Judy Bell. She told me that she "discovered" something which both frightened and worried her, that's why she asked for my help.'

'You ought to pause here, to give time for the leading question: "why send for Dawlish", interpolated Plomley, tidying up the tea table to make room for Dawlish's order which had just arrived.

During the rearrangement of plates and cutlery, Gratton reflected that Plomley had in fact hit the nail on the head—why *had* the girl sent for Dawlish?

'Everybody comes to Dawlish,' said Mrs. Dawlish enigmatically.

Her husband looked at her with a half-apologetic smile. 'Certainly now and again someone in a jam thinks that I might be able to help them to get out of it, but nine times out of ten I refer them to the police, having no love of crime for its own sake. Sometimes—'

'The great mind sees a problem worthy of its own attention,' said Plomley.

'You see, they're both at it,' said Dawlish. 'So I shall leave Felicity to go on with the story.'

His wife took it up readily. 'It really doesn't take much telling. Judy came to Pat and told him she was frightened out of her wits. She was convinced that two attempts had been made on her life, but was afraid to go to the police. Yes, I know,' added Mrs. Dawlish, 'that's what makes nonsense of it, but the obvious conclusion was that she was being blackmailed and both Pat and I thought we ought to find out more, if we could.'

'For once, you're as much to blame as I,' said Dawlish, with evident satisfaction.

'The plan or plot was simple,' Mrs. Dawlish continued, completely ignoring him. 'The man who so frightened Judy had made an appointment with her for one day at the beginning of last week. Pat was to hide in the room and hear what he had to say. But—' Mrs. Dawlish paused—'she disappeared.'

'Disappeared?' echoed Gratton.

'Like Freddie,' murmured Dawlish. 'She didn't turn up for the audition. Curious thing though, the man did. He denied absolutely, using threats or violence against the person of Judy Bell; said in fact, that it was she who had begged him to meet her. You can imagine, can't you, that we were rather—intrigued.'

'I can,' said Gratton warmly.

'And Pat isn't quite a fool at this kind of thing,' Felicity put in frankly. 'He'd taken the precaution of stationing a friend of his outside the flat to follow the man home. He was knocked over the head—the friend, not the man he followed—and when he came round his quarry had left his home and we haven't found him since.'

'The quarry's name,' said Dawlish, 'being Paul.'

'Quite a disappearing act,' said Plomley. 'Hi! waitress!'

It flashed across Gratton's mind that there might not be a single word of truth in the story. It might, indeed, have been made up especially for his benefit. Yet both Dawlish and his wife seemed genuine.

'I may also add,' said Dawlish pleasantly, 'that, according to Judy, at least two attempts have been made to kill her. So, naturally we are anxious to find her.' He stirred his tea vigorously. 'That's where Plomley came in. Three weeks ago, when we first heard of Judy—it was known that a member of this club was implicated. One Freddie Appleyard, in fact. Plomley undertook to keep an eye on him. Mind you, we've nothing against Freddie; we only know that he's one of Judy Bell's few friends. We had a telephone message from Judy this morning. She said she was going to be here this afternoon. So Plomley brought us along for a cup of tea and a quiet chat. The next thing I heard was my car on the move, and rushing out to see what was happening, there was Judy coolly driving away in it!—well, you know the rest. Undoubtedly two men pushed that branch across the road to hold us up and therefore to help her to get away.'

Mrs. Dawlish looked intently at Gratton. 'What do you make of all this, Mr. Gratton?'

Gratton did not immediately answer.

He was aware that all three of them were looking at him anxiously. It was strange to feel that they were waiting on his words. Even Plomley could not hide his anxiety.

But none of them prompted him.

He finished his tea and put the cup down carefully in the saucer.

'I don't know whether I've got it straight or not,' he said, 'but you think that Judy Bell might have gone off on her own accord or might have been—kidnapped.' He couldn't prevent the last word coming out rather shrilly. 'That's about the size of it, isn't it? And you're afraid that Freddie Appleyard might have had something to do with her disappearance. Am I right or wrong?' he demanded.

Mrs. Dawlish said:

'You can't ask for more than that, Pat.'

'I certainly can't,' agreed Dawlish warmly. 'The question is, did she go of her own free will, did she come to meet me and see someone here who frightened her away, or is she leading me up the garden path? There is a fourth alternative—was she forced to go? Not to begin with, for she certainly stole my car by herself. But what happened on the road—was she held up and forced to go with men who might be friends of this Paul? You may be able to help us,' he added, 'something happened here before we turned up, didn't it?'

Gratton knew that he could not keep the story to himself any longer.

*   *   *

The Dawlishes and Plomley listened with rapt attention to his recital of the discovery of the girl and her flight from the dressing-room.

Most of the people in the room had left their tables by this time. Some had gone into the card room, some had left the club, three or four were gathered about the bar, Speck sat at his table, reading a newspaper.

'Hmm,' said Dawlish, when Gratton had finished. 'Remarkable. The more I think of it, the more it seems that she saw someone here who frightened her away.'

'I don't agree,' said Gratton. 'Someone—and I don't believe Freddie would have done it—tied her up and nearly suffocated her with that towel, and I'm sure of one thing—she didn't see anyone after I'd released her.'

'You can't be sure,' said Dawlish. 'She was left alone in the dressing-room. She might have looked out of the window and seen someone coming towards the club-house. She may even have heard a voice which scared her. We can say one thing for certain, however, someone knew or discovered that she was coming here and wanted to prevent her from having a chat with me. I don't think we've proved intent to murder. Whoever did it just bundled her into that locker—she told you it was a fat man, didn't she?'

'Yes, and Freddie—'

Dawlish shrugged. 'Even that may not be true. She may have wanted you to think it was a fat man. Freddie's disappearance is another queer one.'

Gratton said slowly: 'I suppose you know what you're doing, but—well, an attempt *was* made to crash us and the girl *was* assaulted; the police certainly ought to know about it—especially since she's disappeared. I'm prepared to leave that to you, but—Freddie going off is a different matter. I don't see what we can do about that but go to the police.'

'I've telephoned a friend who will find out if Freddie's at his flat or at one of his other haunts,' said Dawlish. 'I certainly don't fancy going to the police.'

Gratton said:

'But it doesn't make sense!' The real enormity of the situation was only now dawning on him. 'How can you possibly handle this without going to the police? What right have you? It's not as if nothing criminal's been done. The more I think about it—'

'The more orthodox you become,' said Dawlish. 'Well, we're in your hands. I don't want the police because Judy was so scared of telling them. She may have fooled us about a lot of things but she wasn't fooling about that.'

Gratton said obstinately: 'I still don't see that that is any reason for keeping it from the police. No, I'm damned if I do! After all, that's what they're for.'

'Well don't get worked up about it,' said Plomley, 'Dawlish hasn't raised any objection, has he?'

'What would make you feel you could leave it to us?' asked Dawlish.

'Proof that the girl and Freddie are all right,' said Gratton.

Dawlish glanced at his watch. 'Right. It's nearly a quarter to five. If we haven't had word by half-past five, then use your own judgment. Do you agree?'

'Well, that's reasonable enough,' admitted Gratton.

Now that he was thinking clearly, however, he wondered if it were reasonable. In another three-quarters of an hour the girl might be taken fifty or sixty miles further away and the task of the police be greatly complicated. After the way she had behaved he might feel that she asked for all she got, but—he could not forget the way she had rested in his arms.

'I'd like you to tell us a little more about Freddie,' said Dawlish. 'Is it true that he does little or nothing for a living?'

'Yes,' said Gratton slowly. 'I think he enjoys lazing about, and he can afford to. He's a bit of a character, but I just can't believe he would get mixed up in a business like this. The more I think of it—'

Dawlish jerked his head up. 'Listen!'

Into the silence came the sound of a car.

'I think I know that engine,' said Dawlish. The car turned into the parking place, and he stood up quickly. 'Let's go and make sure.'

All four of them made for the door, but Dawlish quickly outpaced them.

Yes, the Bentley was there—and Dawlish was walking towards it, hiding the driver. Gratton raised his hands helplessly, Mrs. Dawlish drew alongside him.

'So he was right,' she said.

'Isn't he always right?' asked Plomley.

Dawlish moved, and Gratton saw that the driver was Freddie!

CHAPTER FIVE

GRATTON MAKES A DECISION

Freddie blinked up at the four people who descended on him.

'Well,' said Dawlish, in a deep voice.

'Not well at all,' said Freddie. 'Brrrh, I'm cold. 'Lo, Toby. Sorry about the game. Can explain it all.' He grinned. 'Mind if I get out, Colossus?'

'Mind explaining what you're doing in my car?' demanded Dawlish.

'Yours? Lucky man,' declared Freddie, opening the door. 'Goes like a bird. Brrrh!' he repeated, beating his arms about his chest as he climbed down, 'it's like midwinter. And what a wind. I'm going to get something hot to drink.'

'You're going to stay right here until you've explained what you're doing in my car,' said Dawlish.

Freddie looked up at him. He was a small man; and looked more so in comparison with Dawlish. His cheek bones were high, his cheeks hollow, his dark hair waved thinly in the wind.

'Have a heart, it's raining,' he protested. 'And no umbrella for the lady.'

'What—' began Dawlish.

'Oh, all right, I'll tell you,' said Freddie. 'Simple, really. I thought I was being clever. Judy Bell turned up at the club after lunch. I hurried out to see her—hence no blazer,' he added sadly. 'Bumped into a fat man. The smiling type. Judy wasn't there. "Will you tell me what the hell you're doing on enclosed premises?" I asked, and—believe it or not—he planted a fist as big as a shoulder of mutton right in my bread-basket. Ooch! There appeared to be two of them, and the second brigand, whom I shall call Karloff, lifted me like a sack of potatoes, and dumped me into a car standing outside in the road. He also tied a bag over my head. Joking apart,' said Freddie earnestly, 'I was scared of that gent. Nasty manner with him. Well there I sat till Fatty came out. There was a brief exchange of pleasantries, then Fatty took the wheel and off we went, stopping only to dump me behind a haystack a few miles away. Later, they came back, resumed the journey and I was dumped in the Bentley and told to take a message to a Mr. Patrick Dawlish.'

He looked round inquiringly, and Dawlish nodded.

'Mission about to be discharged,' said Freddie. 'Message reads: Tell Dawlish if he consults police Judy will be no more. Message ends. Bit of a snifter, isn't it?'

Gratton did not argue any further. He was convinced that Freddie would not have faked such a message; although he half-suspected that Dawlish believed Freddie knew more about the girl than he had acknowledged. The club-room was now almost deserted, and they sat in a corner going over the situation again for Freddie's benefit. He appeared to be appalled at Judy Bell's plight.

'Thing is, what to do?' he demanded.

'We'll decide on that later,' said Dawlish. 'It looks as if the fat man and his companion were the pair who nearly caused our spill, Gratton. They must have stopped by that haystack and watched the road, seen Judy driving along, and arranged the fallen branch to stop her. She—'

'Well, it didn't stop her,' Gratton said obstinately, 'the Bentley was driven right over it.'

'And it still goes,' said Freddie.

'You take all this pretty calmly,' said Dawlish.

'Nothing else to do.' Freddie said airily. 'Bad business, but the great Dawlish has my confidence. I knew Judy was in a bit of a spot, although she wouldn't tell me what. Matter of fact—' he grinned. 'I suggested that she should come to see you. Toby, old chap, I think we ought to leave it to Dawlish for the time being. He knows his way about and we are as children in affairs of civil violence. One condition, though: that we help.' He lifted a questioning eyebrow at Gratton, who nodded. 'Condition accepted, Dawlish?'

'Yes,' said Dawlish quietly.

'All settled, then,' said Freddie comfortably. Now I suppose you want me to lead you to the spot where I was detained.'

'Can you?'

'Blindfolded. I know this country.'

'All right, I'll take your word for it. My wife and I will leave right away, and I'll be at the haystack at eight o'clock tonight. There's a moon, and if the clouds clear we'll be able to see fairly well.'

It was a clear, moonlight night with just enough wind to stir the trees near the haystack where Gratton and Freddie waited. To Gratton, there was something unreal about the whole affair, unreal about the way he had driven, at Freddie's suggestion, the long way round to reach this spot; unreal, to leave the car a hundred yards away and finish the journey on foot; unreal to be standing and waiting here. It was five minutes to eight.

'Jumpy?'

'I am rather.'

'My heart's beating like a steam-hammer, too,' confessed Freddie. 'Better not smoke,' he added as Gratton took out his cigarette case, 'in the words of the master, we may be watched.'

That added to the creepiness of the night and of their being here.

Minutes dragged by . . .

He thought of what Freddie had told him about Dawlish. A remarkable story. He was 'the' Dawlish; famous for his work of counter-espionage in England; a man who had hit the headlines several times when he had taken part in the investigation of serious crimes. A man, moreover, who knew the police well and would not have kept this affair from them unless he was certain that the risk was justified. He had a flair for investigation which even the police had acknowledged. Freddie had been so sure that he would be interested that he had confidently sent Judy to him.

All he said about Judy was that he had known her for several years—their families had lived in the same country town. They were not close friends, he made haste to add; Judy had been brought up to be suspicious of 'friends'; a disadvantage peculiar to heiresses.

'Eight o'clock,' Gratton announced suddenly.

The only sound was the murmuring of wind. No traffic had passed during the last ten minutes. They stood in the shadow of the haystack, and could see for miles in the mellow moonlight.

'I wish—' began Gratton.

A figure loomed up beside him. It was Dawlish.

'Must you scare the lights out of me?' demanded Gratton, peevishly.

Freddie chuckled.

'Sure you can find your way to that copse?' Dawlish asked him.

'Sceptical beggar, aren't you?' complained Freddie. 'Of course I'm sure. Just follow me.'

They left the shadow of the haystack and moved quietly towards a gate which led to a by-road. Freddie made little sound, Gratton seemed to be plunging about like an elephant, but Dawlish made neither comment or complaint. Nevertheless, he appeared to be afraid that they were being watched. His fear, if that word could be applied to him, passed itself on to Gratton. He stared nervously at the shadowed trees, frightened that someone might jump out of the darkness upon them. Far beyond them he could see a house on the hill; lights shining from two windows.

They reached an open gateway.

'In here,' Freddie said, *sotto voce.*

Dawlish said: 'By the way, do remember that if anything happens—and it's my bet that it will—don't shout. Is that clear?'

'Soft muted voices on the gentle night,' murmured Freddie. 'Cheerful chap, aren't you? Well, here we are. This is the spot.'

At his words, a vivid beam of light shone straight at them. Gratton's heart thumped.

Dawlish had expected this, had known—

'Don't move, any of you.'

The voice came from behind them, and when Gratton became more accustomed to the light, he saw several men stepping from the trees. Each held a weapon.

With a violent leap, Freddie jumped to one side, but as he moved, one of the men struck him a powerful blow on the side of the face. Freddie toppled over.

'I thought you had *some* sense, Dawlish.' The words came

from a very fat man carrying a pistol. 'You were crazy to come here. I take it you want to know where Judy is?'

'That's on the agenda, certainly,' agreed Dawlish.

'She's a long way from here,' sneered the other.

'You'd be a fool if she weren't,' said Dawlish.

'Think so? Well, walk straight on—follow the man in front, and if you give any trouble we'll shoot. Get going.' He moved rapidly to Freddie, who was staggering to his feet. 'Don't let's have any more nonsense from you,' he growled. 'Hurry!'

Freddie looked at him coolly, then turned and followed Gratton and Dawlish.

Gratton felt dumbstruck. At least five men had been waiting for them in the copse and it was not reassuring to know that Dawlish had half-expected it. Could he have anticipated so many men? Had this gone to plan? Gratton himself had expected Dawlish to turn the tables swiftly, he had come to think that the big man was infallible, now he knew the folly of such blind trust. Did the fat man intend to kill—?

Gratton remembered with a shudder of fear, Judy's corpse-like face when he had released her; and the branch across the road.

Suddenly Dawlish stumbled.

As he fell, a man leapt from behind a tree and struck at him. He heard Dawlish gasp and saw him crash down. The man struck again. Gratton swung round and rushed towards the copse, hoping that Freddie was beside him. If they could get into the heart of the copse there would be a chance to get away, they could hide until morning, they—

He tripped, and as he fell forward something crashed on the back of his head and he lost consciousness.

CHAPTER SIX

THREE IN THE PARLOUR

Gratton came round slowly. He heard nothing, and for some seconds he did not realise what had happened. Gradually recollection returned. Well, at least he was alive.

He was in no shape to think clearly, however, to apportion blame to Dawlish for leading them into a trap. It was all he could do to lift his head and look about him. He was in a small, dimly lit room. Dawlish was lying on the floor breathing heavily. There was no sign of Freddie.

Where was he? How long had he been here? Dawlish's breathing was steady, but the big man did not move. Hard to understand that a man with such a reputation had just walked into this.

He jerked his head up.

A scream pierced the silence, from someone not far away. It shuddered through the air making Gratton feel icily cold, and the ensuing silence all the more intense. He waited in terror for the sound to be repeated.

There it was!

Perspiration broke out on his forehead. Now all was silent

again but there was no mistaking the scream. It seemed to come from the next room. He stared at the blank wall, desperately frightened. Dawlish did not stir. Gratton stood up; the shock of the scream had cleared his head, but he was unsteady as he crossed to Dawlish.

'Dawlish,' he muttered.

'*No, no, no!*' a man cried. 'I can't stand it, I can't stand it, don't do it. *Don't do it!*'

Was that Freddie?

He couldn't be sure; nor could he recognise the voice; but he could hear the words clearly—and now he heard a second voice.

'How much did Dawlish tell you?'

'Nothing—nothing at all.'

The scream came again, and into the silence which followed came the question in a quiet voice:

'How much did Dawlish tell you?'

'Nothing—I swear it!' Now Gratton could hear the man's heavy breathing, he was gasping for breath.

Another pause; Gratton steeled himself for the scream, but all he heard was a muttering, gibbering sound. And then the quiet-voiced man spoke again.

'We'll try the other fellow.'

The movements stopped. Every moment Gratton expected the door to this room to open, but there was only the sinister silence.

Then *Dawlish spoke* softly.

'Steady, Gratton.'

Gratton started. 'You—you're awake.'

Dawlish did not move his head, and spoke very softly.

'Yes, I heard it. Keep steady. Tell them everything you know, there's no need to keep anything back. You'll be all right.'

Gratton gasped: 'They—they've tortured him, they—'

'They'll try anything,' said Dawlish. 'Take it easy, old chap. And Freddie was probably bluffing them, they couldn't make him yell like that unless he wanted to. They're easy to bluff, you know.'

His reassuring voice made Gratton feel ashamed of his outburst. He began to make excuses for himself. To come round with an aching head and that awful sense of fear, to hear the screaming and the obvious sounds of torture—was it any wonder he had cracked?

Gratton swung round. The door had opened silently and a man stood on the threshold. He jerked his head towards the passage, and Gratton moved towards him.

He saw that another man stood behind the first. Together they seized his arms and hustled him along to the room from which Gratton had heard the voices. He gritted his teeth and shook himself free. He was determined not to show weakness now, and to hide his fear.

He narrowed his eyes against the bright light in the next room.

The first man he saw was the fat fellow; and another, smaller man with a grotesquely ugly face stood by his chair. The room was otherwise empty. As Gratton entered, the man lifted a glass and tossed down a drink.

'You'd better talk,' he said. 'Take him over there.'

Gratton looked 'over there'.

The sight would have turned a weaker stomach; for the wall was splashed with blood, a bloodstained towel was lying on the floor and there were little pools of blood on a small glass-topped table.

Gratton clenched his teeth but managed to step towards the chair without any show of feeling.

The fat man drew on his cigar, and let the smoke curl from

his lips as he stared at Gratton. Perhaps because the nearness of danger had heightened his sense of perception, Gratton noted every feature, every tiny peculiarity of the fat man's face. A diamond ring on the little finger of his right hand, with which he held the cigar, glittered beneath a bright light which was suspended between them.

The fat man did not speak for a while, and Gratton forced himself to keep his composure; this was all part of the trick; they were wearing on his nerves. No time to think of the appalling wickedness of it, to marvel that such a thing could happen in England, and that he was now at these people's mercy.

Suddenly, the light dropped until it was only a few inches from Gratton's eyes, blinding him.

'They're up to all the tricks' Dawlish had said.

The fat man spoke in a soft voice.

'Gratton, what did Dawlish tell you?'

Gratton was too startled by the suddenness of the question to answer. The fat man leaned forward, and his voice seemed even gentler.

'Gratton, you're going to answer all our questions, whether you like it or not. Better make it easy for yourself. What did Dawlish tell you?'

'What—what about?' asked Gratton. The words came out abruptly, he had difficulty in keeping his lips steady.

'You know what about,' said the fat man. 'Did he tell the police?'

'No!'

'You seem very sure of that,' said the fat man, 'and it isn't easy to be sure of anything Dawlish says or does. How do you know?'

'I wanted him to,' said Gratton. He must speak more steadily, more calmly, his words mustn't come out like bullet shots. 'I tried to persuade him to, if—'

'Go on,' murmured the fat man.

'If Appleyard hadn't come back with that message I'd have told the police myself. Dawlish was against it, he—he thought he could handle this alone.'

'Ah,' said the fat man, 'so Dawlish is running true to form. He always thinks he can do better than the police.' He gave a little satisfied chuckle. 'So my message made you change your mind, Gratton. But before you received that you argued with Dawlish, didn't you?'

'I—'

'You were *seen* arguing with him,' said the fat man. 'Don't think you can get away with lies, Gratton. Appleyard made the same mistake, and he will rue it for many a long day. What did he tell you?'

Dawlish had said that he could tell the whole story, but—wouldn't it seem too easy? Would the fat man be satisfied? Wouldn't it be better to hesitate, to pretend reluctance? Gratton sat quite still, without speaking. Curiously enough he was calmer and more confident now. He felt that he could submit himself to some pain; that it would be wise to allow himself to be hurt, because it would seem much more convincing when he talked.

And he had been seen arguing with Dawlish; by someone in the club-room. So—the fat man had a spy there!

A clink of steel made him look round. 'Karloff' was holding one of the blood-stained instruments; a scalpel.

'What did he tell you?' repeated the fat man.

'It—it was all such a muddle,' Gratton said, 'first the girl—'

'Never mind her, and don't run away with the idea that it will help you if you gain time, Gratton. Now, if you don't answer immediately—'

He smiled; a faint twist of his rosebud of a mouth.

Next moment, the light flashed down in front of Gratton's eyes again and he reared back involuntarily. He had forgotten that trick, and it made his heart race. When the light was removed, there seemed to be two fat faces instead of one, moving in and out, one face superimposed on the other.

'Well!' barked the man.

'He told me—'

The story came out, haltingly; Gratton could only remember it in snatches, relieved that he could do this without letting Dawlish down—or Freddie—or the girl. *She* was here, in the hands of these men; it didn't bear thinking about.

'I see,' said the fat man when he had finished. 'I think perhaps you have been wise, Gratton, and told the truth—this agrees very nearly with what I already know. Dawlish didn't use any other argument to persuade you against going to the police? He gave no hint of *why* this is happening, *why* Judy Bell is so frightened?'

'He said he didn't know.'

'It will be good for Dawlish not to know,' the fat man said complacently. 'He was beginning to think he was infallible.' He chuckled. 'But I haven't quite finished with you yet, Gratton. How many men did Dawlish bring with him?'

Gratton stared blankly.

'Now don't pretend not to know,' murmured the fat man. 'How many—'

'He was alone!'

'Now, come,' protested the fat man, 'you can't expect me to believe that. Dawlish is a fool in some ways but he wouldn't venture on a mission like this with only you and Appleyard to help him. He and his wife and the man Plomley left the club-house for London at twenty minutes to six—what time did he return and how many people did he bring with him?'

'I tell you he was alone!' snapped Gratton.

Out of the corner of his eyes he could see the scalpel glinting in Karloff's hand.

'*He was alone!*' Gratton cried desperately. 'We met him at the haystack, he said he'd be there at eight o'clock, he was there to the minute. I tell you he was alone!'

The fat man looked at Karloff.

'What *is* the report?' he asked.

Karloff shrugged his shoulders.

'No one was seen outside.'

'I see.' The fat man took the cigar from his lips again and contemplated the ash. 'I *see*,' he repeated. 'Perhaps Dawlish *has* been foolish enough to come without his usual helpers. We mustn't take it for granted, but it's possible. Gratton, if you have lied to me I shall find out about it, and you will regret that you didn't tell me the whole truth. Was Dawlish awake when you left the room?' The question came abruptly.

'He—he was muttering to himself,' said Gratton. 'I thought he was talking to me, but he was rambling.'

Another exchange of glances between the two men convinced him that he had been right to say that.

Was this all they wanted now?

His glance fell on the blood-stained towel and he thought of Freddie. He gritted his teeth again; now he felt a new emotion, fear had gone, and in its place was a wild anger against the men who could do these things, who might have disfigured Freddie for life. And they had the girl in their power. If he moved now, while their attention was distracted he might—

What was the use of thinking like that? There were other men outside. One could do nothing at all against so many. But the anger remained—less wild now, becoming a deep, burning hatred.

'Very well,' said the fat man abruptly. 'Take him away. And remember, Gratton—if you've lied you'll come back.'

A man at the door took charge of him and led him along a narrow low-ceilinged passage.

He turned the corner.

The door of a room was open, and he saw a man lying on a camp bed—a man whose shirt looked to be a mass of blood. His eyes were closed, his beaked nose unmistakable. It was Freddie—

Gratton reared up.

'I want—' he began hoarsely.

His guard pushed him brutally along the passage, past the door. But Gratton could not get that picture out of his mind's eye. There was no doubt at all that it was Freddie, lying there unconscious, perhaps near death. He thought desperately of attacking the guard; and as if the man understood what he was thinking, a gun was pressed against his ribs. He might have made an attempt then, but another man appeared at the end of a second passage.

The newcomer flung open a door, then stood aside. Gratton was pushed into the room, the door was closed, and he heard the key turn in the lock.

CHAPTER SEVEN

A MAN SAYS 'HALLO'

The room was small and barely furnished. Along one wall was a camp bed, and at the head a small table on which stood a clock, ticking loudly—the only sound that Gratton could hear except his own breathing. Religious texts hung on the walls.

He couldn't think clearly; the only picture in his mind was that of Freddie. Oh, it was no use blaming Dawlish for everything, although the man was to blame for most of this. The fool, to walk blindly into such a trap! As for being a fool—what price he, Tobias Gratton, for not insisting on telling the police? One telephone call—thirty seconds' conversation—and the whole ghastly business could have been avoided. Instead Dawlish had dissuaded him, and disaster had come.

Would he ever be allowed to leave the place alive?

It was time he came to grips with the problem. Obviously something was at stake so large, so important, that a gang of criminals would go to the extreme limit to get what they wanted. What had led up to it was unimportant; what part Judy Bell played hardly mattered now. What were his chances of escape and of getting Freddie away.

He didn't think of Dawlish; the giant could look after himself. But it would be impossible to leave without Freddie, unless—his heart leapt at the thought—there was a hope of getting away and fetching help.

He stood quite still, staring at the door, but there was no sound of movement.

He went to the window, and experimentally tweaked the curtain—and found himself gazing at a wooden shutter!

His disappointment was so acute that he groaned as he turned away. So they had taken every precaution; no light would shine out, he could do nothing to attract attention.

He went back to the bed.

As he sat down, he heard a key inserted in the lock, but he was too dispirited to look up. The door opened and a man came in, carrying a tray with a glass, small bottle and a jug of water.

'Don't get drunk,' he advised, and cackled with laughter.

Gratton had never needed a drink so desperately; and yet he sat there until the door was closed and locked again. He couldn't understand this; why should they let him have a drink. Thirst overwhelmed him.

He poured a finger of whisky, sniffed it, added a little water and drank it slowly. He leaned back against the wall, finished the drink and poured out another. For ten minutes he sat like that, and when he opened his eyes he looked at the shuttered window with more than a ray of hope.

After all, the shutter was only made of wood.

He got up again and examined it more closely. Yes, it was of thick wood. He tapped it, getting a dull, hollow sound. Perhaps it wasn't so thick as he had imagined. He looked for the screws which held it in position; but he saw nothing. Queer. He examined it more closely. Now he discovered that it was fitted from the outside; the window had been boarded up, and short of smashing it or sawing it, there was no way of removing the shutter from the inside. So he'd had it. He shrugged his shoulders. No sense in tormenting himself about that possibility, his only hope now lay in overpowering the guard next time the door was opened. One against—how many would he have to tackle? Half a dozen at least and possibly more, all of them armed. On the other hand, if he pulled it off, he would be able to take the guard's gun. It was surprising what one desperate armed man could do.

Steady! The key was being inserted again!

Gratton stepped hastily to the wall behind the door. He held the bottle like a club, and stared at the handle, waiting for it to turn. Ah! The lock turned, now was the moment. He raised the bottle.

The door opened an inch.

'*Hallo*,' a man whispered.

It was a soft, husky voice, nothing like the guard's. Was this a trick, an attempt to make him attack so that they had an excuse for beating him up?

'Hallo, there!' called the unseen man. A pause, and then: 'Pat, are you in there?'

Pat! Dawlish's christian name!

'Who's that?' whispered Gratton.

The door opened wider and a man slipped through. He gave an expansive grin as he closed it behind him.

'You're Gratton, I take it?'

'Yes, but—'

'Claude. Friend of Dawlish,' said the newcomer. 'They haven't knocked you about, anyhow. What's that you've got in your hand—damme, they haven't been feasting you!'

Gratton said with an effort: 'They gave me a drink. What are you doing—'

'Broke in. The fat oaf didn't bargain for a super cracksman—that's me.' He ran his fingers through untidy bushy brown hair. 'Do you know where Pat is?'

'In—in another room,' said Gratton, faintly.

'Oh, my dear fellow. One presumes that. Nasty, draughty places, passages are, with lots of doors. The question is, which room? No hurry.'

'There's the devil of a hurry!' snapped Gratton.

'Oh well, perhaps you're right. Might as well finish one job at a time though.'

Moving very swiftly, he opened the door and darted into the passage. Gratton saw him bend down; the next moment the stranger was pulling a man into the room, feet first.

'Hold the door open, old chap,' said Claude, reproachfully. 'Fellow's got wide shoulders.'

Gratton pulled the door back.

The victim, unconscious, and breathing heavily, was his guard.

'Thanks,' said Claude. 'He must weigh fourteen stone. Heaviest job I've tackled since I had to get Pat out of a fan-light.' He went down on one knee and felt the man's pulse. 'Steadyish,' he said. 'Haven't a clothes line or a nice length of rope in your pocket, have you?'

Gratton shook his head impatiently. 'We can lock him in.'

'Certainly we can. Trouble is, this merchant has a voice and said voice can raise a hell of a stinkum if we let him use it. What about the curtains?' Claude strode across the room, stretched up and pulled the curtains down.

They tore easily, and soon he had half a dozen strips. Gratton watched the man in fascination.

Claude looked up.

'Any use at tying knots? Have a go at his legs, will you? Mind he doesn't kick. He's not so blotto as you think he is.'

Together they bound and gagged the guard, then stood up as one man.

'Nice drill,' said Claude. 'Like a gun?' He dipped his hand into his pocket, took out an automatic and tossed it to Gratton. 'That's mine,' Claude told him. He took a heavy Luger from his pocket. 'This belonged to our friend in distress. Seen Judy?'

'No,' said Gratton, 'Freddie and—'

'Pat,' completed Claude. 'What a man! Ready to sacrifice his life *and* yours for the sake of this little mystery. Can't quite understand what he's up to, but he doesn't often put a foot wrong. But I wish we could find Judy. Not much likelihood that she's here, I suppose.'

He looked about the room, examining the walls, paying marked attention to the window, and also to the lock of the door. That finished, he went down on his knees and ran through the unconscious man's pockets. He took out a handful of odds and ends, but none of them seemed to interest him. He put them in a neat pile by the man's head.

'What a shock he'll get when he comes round,' said Claude. 'Well, ready for the sortie?'

'It's about time,' said Gratton.

'Hmm, yes. Any idea of total numbers?'

'I've seen five different men.'

'Double it,' said Claude. For a moment he looked serious; his eyes narrowed, his manner became calculating. 'Tim and Ted are outside, making us four. What's happened since you've been here?'

'Absolute ruddy chaos!' declared Gratton.

Claude grinned.

Gratton told him briefly what had happened from the time that he had come round. At the account of the blood-stained table and towel, and the sight of Freddie on the camp bed, Claude's lips tightened; he looked cool and dangerous.

Gratton had heard nothing, but suddenly Claude stood quite still, staring at the door. After a long pause, a key sounded in the lock. Claude flattened himself to one side of the door and gestured to Gratton to do the same on the other.

Gratton saw that he had the gun in his hand like a club, holding it by the barrel. He turned his automatic. At last he was in a position to attack.

The door opened wide.

'Joe—' the newcomer began, and then he saw the guard stretched out on the floor. He opened his mouth to shout, but Claude jumped at him and spread his left hand over his face. It was a swift, frightening attack, and the man reeled back. Gratton moved forward swiftly and brought the butt of the gun down on the newcomer's head.

'*Very* nice work,' congratulated Claude, 'but we'll have to be quick, he may have been sent along to see what had happened to poor old Joe.' He picked up three lengths of curtain, and tossed one to Gratton.

In less than five minutes, the second man was bound and gagged.

From the newcomer's pocket, Claude took a bunch of keys. He slipped them into his own pocket.

'They were worth waiting for,' he said. 'Freedom of the palace, so to speak. Seen this shanty from the outside?'

Gratton shook his head.

'Annexe or whatnot to the big house. Two main passages, two doors, I came in at a window which they were foolish enough to leave unguarded. Lights at three rooms, including this one. Ready?'

Claude stepped into the passage ahead of Gratton. The only light came from the room they were leaving, but he appeared to be in no doubt as to which way to turn. Gratton found himself retracing his footsteps. Very soon they would come upon the room where he had seen Freddie.

The door was locked.

'Know anything about this?' whispered Claude.

'Freddie—'

'Will keep,' declared Claude. 'Sorry, but there we are. Next room?'

'That's where Fryer—'

'Torture chamber,' said Claude. 'Come on.' They walked softly towards the door. 'Dawlish had his turn yet?'

'He was to follow me.'

'Hmm. No light under the door,' said Claude. He opened it cautiously. All was silence. Holding the gun steadily, he switched on a beam of light.

'Flown,' he said dramatically. 'Inquisition and whatnot still on show, but no Fryer. Odd. What's next door?'

'The room where I woke up.'

'Sleeping chamber,' said Claude.

There were no lights under the door of that room, either, and Claude repeated his manoeuvre, although with less abandon. The room was also empty. They stood on the threshold. No sound disturbed the quiet. The silence was uncanny.

Claude did not immediately return to Freddie's room, however, but looked into the 'torture-chamber'. Gratton, seething with impatience, watched him dab a finger in a pool of blood.

'What on earth are you up to now?' he demanded. 'Haven't we enough to do without—'

Claude looked at him:

'Not blood, I think. Ink. They must have staged a dress-rehearsal.'

CHAPTER EIGHT

DRESS REHEARSAL?

Gratton looked at the thin red liquid which had helped to put the fear of death into him. Yes, it was ink.

'Silly, isn't it?' asked Claude. 'A little hint of what they might do, if they're driven to it, though. Let's see Freddie.'

Claude led the way briskly along the passage. He made no attempt to keep quiet as he opened the door to Freddie's room.

Freddie still lay on the bed—

Claude bent over the unconscious man and raised one eyelid; then rolled up Freddie's right sleeve. Half-way up the forearm was a small red patch, and in the centre of it a puncture.

'Looks as if he's had a shot of morphia,' he muttered. 'Not much doubt about it—nor that the birds have flown.'

'It's incredible!'

'I wouldn't say that,' objected Claude. 'I think Fryer tumbled to the fact that we were close at hand, and couldn't be sure how many of us there were. Rum show, though.' He looked at the boarded window. 'I don't think there's any more danger, but we may as well stick together.'

They made a complete tour of the bungalow.

There were three rooms in the other passage, all filled with empty show cases. Could the building have been used for a museum? The back door was bolted on the inside.

'So they went out the front way, taking Pat with 'em, I suppose,' said Claude. 'Still, it could be worse.' He unbolted the back door, and to Gratton's astonishment, opened his mouth and emitted a shrill cry which startled him by its likeness to the hoot of an owl. He repeated it three times, then waited; but no answering cry came.

'No luck,' he said at last, 'or rather, plenty of luck. Ted and Tim—'

'Who *are* Ted and Tim?'

'More friends of Dawlish,' said Claude promptly. He leaned against the door, digging his hands into his pockets and taking out a cigarette case with one hand and a light with the other. 'Smoke? What happened, of course, is that Fryer got scared, as I said, and Tim and Ted have followed him, so Pat isn't alone. There is, of course, the risk that Tim and Ted were spotted and nobbled, although I can't believe it. Listen!'

Again he showed that uncanny sense of hearing, and Gratton felt his pulse racing. Gradually, he became aware of the sound of a car. Soon the glow of headlights appeared and shone upon the big grey house.

'And they're expected,' said Claude. 'Lights are going up.' For the first time yellow lights appeared at the windows of the house, which was only a few hundred yards away. Men climbed out of the car—and one of them was in police uniform.

'Hal-lo!' exclaimed Claude. 'It looks as if the police *were* warned. Let's get out of here. Come on!' he snapped, as Gratton hesitated, 'we don't want 'em to find us.'

'But surely we ought—'

'To get Freddie away,' said Claude. 'Chief bargaining weapon with Fryer is—no police.'

He was crisp and authoritative.

Gratton did not argue.

Claude hoisted the unconscious man over his shoulder, and without a word, they walked along the passage to the front door.

'How are we going to get away?'

'Tootsies for a start,' said Claude, 'and then by car.'

They left the path, and walked over uneven meadowland towards a hedge which showed up tall and dark in the moonlight.

Gratton was the first to see the gate, which stood open. They walked through it to a narrow, rutted lane. The hedges were high on either side, the darkness profound.

Peering, with many false hopes, they at last espied the outlines of a car. 'Now we won't be long,' Claude said cheerfully, 'We'll put Freddie in the back, and I'll take the wheel. Here—hold him a minute!' he exclaimed, in sudden urgency.

'What—'

'Hist!'

'May I know what you gentlemen are doing here?' asked a solemn voice out of the gloom. 'And what may you be carrying, sir?'

'Carrying?' squeaked Claude.

'That's right, sir, carrying.'

A constable stepped forward, while Gratton stood helpless with Freddie over his shoulder, and Claude seemed too flabbergasted for speech.

They could now see him clearly; even to the whistle he was raising to his lips.

'*So* sorry,' said Claude.

He drove his fist into the policeman's stomach, and as the unhappy constable lurched forward, struck him sharply on the jaw.

'Good heavens! You—'

'Get Freddie inside!' snapped Claude. 'We can't risk being caught now. Confound it, it would mean six months at least! And you'd be an accessory.' By the time Gratton had put Freddie into the back, the engine was turning over.

'They'll trace the car!' whispered Gratton urgently, 'he'll have taken the number—'

'False,' said Claude. 'Don't be such a fusspot. I only hope there aren't any more, lurking about the lane.'

'I tell you this is madness!'

'Of course it is, but we can't undo it now. Get in, man!'

Almost against his will Gratton climbed in beside Claude. As he settled down, he knew that he had committed himself once and for all.

The car moved off.

Claude chuckled.

'Rather funny, what!'

'Not my idea of humour,' said Gratton grimly.

'Oh, come,' protested Claude, 'it isn't often one has a chance to dot a policeman in a good cause, and Judy Bell could very easily be described as a good cause, don't you think?'

Gratton's flat was one of four in a large Victorian house just outside Harrow. It had a separate entrance and was on the ground floor. They reached it half-an-hour after leaving the policeman in the lane. The car was drawn up close to the entrance, and Claude lifted Freddie out. Together they carried him to Gratton's sitting-room. Across one end was a deep sofa, and here they laid him. Claude straightened up with relief.

'How many bedrooms!'

'Two, and—'

'Thanks, I'll stay the night,' said Claude. He grinned,

engagingly. A streak of dirt covered his right cheek and there was another on his forehead. 'Food's too much to hope for, I suppose?'

'I can manage a snack,' said Gratton reluctantly.

'The perfect host! Now if you could rustle up some beer—' He sank into an easy chair.

Gratton opened a cupboard and took out two bottles of light ale.

Claude watched him fill a tankard. 'Ahh!' he breathed, stretching out his hand. 'You know, Gratton, you're one in a thousand. One in *ten* thousands.' He drank deeply. 'One in a million!'

Gratton smoothed his hair down.

'Never mind the eulogies. Tell me simply what all this cloak and dagger stuff. is about.'

'I wish I knew,' said Claude, his face bland with innocence. 'Fact is, Pat's the chap to tell you. He, or one or other of his devoted disciples are sure to ring through before the night's out,' he added. 'What's the time?'

Gratton said, incredulously: 'How can they ring through if they don't know this address, or where you are?'

'Oh, we'd arranged to make this the rendezvous for the night,' Claude assured him airily. 'It's nice and handy, and Pat felt sure he could rely on you. You know, I'm worried about Pat. He walked into it with his eyes wide open, but even he doesn't see everything, and I don't think he intended to be taken away from the museum.'

Gratton said: 'So now it's a museum.'

'Well, show-cases and all that kind of thing round the walls,' said Claude reasonably. 'I think we'll find that the past or present owner once had a private museum and housed it in that bungalow. The question is, was it with the knowledge of the present owner of the grey house that Fryer took it over? I'd say not. In fact I'd say that the said owner discovered there was some funny business afoot, and warned the police. Great Scott!'

He jumped up, nearly upsetting his beer.

'Now what's the matter?' demanded Gratton.

'My dear chap! Those registration plates!' He fled out of the room.

Gratton did not follow him.

He wanted time to think about the situation. Claude was certainly not the fool he pretended to be, and he had casually thrown out several useful and probably accurate theories. Gratton set himself to consider the facts as he knew them.

Judy Bell was in the hands of Fryer; Dawlish presumably had been taken away; the mysterious Tim and Ted might have followed Dawlish—that certainly seemed likely. He, Gratton, had been completely fooled, in order to make him talk; Fryer had not gone as far as murder, but he had used violence and drugs. And—Claude had knocked a policeman out, and was now changing the number plates on his car.

Gratton realised that when he had left the policeman, he had committed himself completely.

He *could* go to the police and tell the whole story, but—no, Judy Bell was worth taking a risk for. And it was obvious that Fryer was nervous of the police, or he would not have left the bungalow so hurriedly.

Claude came in, rubbing his hands. 'Well, that's done.'

In spite of everything, Gratton liked this man; and as he had decided to accept the situation, he may as well be helpful. 'I'll get some food out while you're washing.'

'Good fellow,' said Claude. 'I hope you come into a fortune one day.'

Gratton grinned.

Claude busied himself in the bathroom and Gratton opened a tin of spiced ham, then cut some bread. He was short of bread, but if it came to a point—

He looked at his watch; it was twenty-five minutes past twelve.

So they would have to manage with what bread he had. He supposed it wasn't really surprising that it was so late, considering that he must have been unconscious for an hour or more. At the back of his mind was the thought that Freddie would be round before long and Freddie might be able to tell him more than Dawlish had done or Claude seemed prepared to do.

He carried the laden tray into the living-room. He was lowering it on to a table when the telephone-bell rang.

CHAPTER NINE

WORD FROM THE WEST

The telephone was in the hall.

Gratton rushed out, followed by Claude.

They were an equal distance from the telephone, each with a hand outstretched. The bell rang on monotonously as they paused; then Gratton grabbed.

'I'll take it,' he said.

Claude appeared to slip, knocking against Gratton. When he regained his balance, the receiver had changed hands.

Gratton stood by, fuming.

'Dear old boy,' said Claude, 'of course it's me. Whom else do you think it would be? . . . Eh? . . . Like a Trojan, old boy, a real Trojan . . . No one could have behaved better . . . Let me take the call like a lamb . . . Yes, old boy I'm all ears . . . Now listen, Pat . . .'

'Dawlish!' breathed Gratton.

He could just hear Dawlish's voice, though not what he said. He had been quite sure that Dawlish had been taken away by Fryer. Could he have escaped so quickly? It was almost miraculous.

'Yes, I've got all that, old chap,' Claude went on. 'All perfectly clear, no confusion . . . Take Freddie and Gratton, if they'll play, to Tor House, Merrance, Cornwall . . . Yes, yes, I was coming to that. I'm to take them to the village and they're to *watch* Tor House. Dear old boy, it's already as good as done. Gratton's straining at the leash to go over the top . . . Yes, we may meet Tim and Ted there. Right. And . . . Pat! Pat! What about Felicity?'

Dawlish appeared to be speaking for a long time. When he had finished, Claude drew a deep breath.

'Now, listen, Pat,' he said plaintively, 'I'll do all I can for you, but there are limits. I just daren't face her . . . Of course she'll want to come . . . I'll have to give her the address, it's no use pretending I can keep it from her . . . Pat! *Patrick!*' He took the receiver from his ear and looked at it blankly. 'The devil's rung off,' he cried. 'A dastardly trick!'

Gratton, who had been so pent up with words, could find nothing to say.

'I mean,' said Claude, 'it's a bit much to expect me to grapple with an enraged wife.' He led the way into the sitting-room. 'Well, that's one thing off my mind. Pat's all right.'

'I'm not so sure,' said Gratton.

'My dear old chap! I heard him. You may think I could be mistaken about his voice, but never about the context of his speech. No one in the world but Patrick would have—'

'How did he get away?' demanded Gratton drily.

'*I* don't know,' said Claude.

'Now look here—'

'There wasn't time to go into details on the telephone,' protested Claude, 'we hardly had a minute as it was. He said he followed Fryer to a hotel near Oxford and overheard him planning to go to Tor House. Obviously he's been in touch with Ted and Tim, they may have got him out of Fryer's clutches. Now the scene's moved, too, we're going somewhere west—like the West Country?' He began to sing. 'Tra-la-la—'

'Claude,' said Gratton furiously, 'will you, once and for all, get this into your head. I am not going to be made a fool of by you, Dawlish, his wife, Tim, Ted, Fryer, or the King of Siam. I've had quite enough jiggery-pokery. If you care to talk seriously and stop acting like a Court jester, we might get somewhere, but unless you do—I'm going to telephone the police and tell them everything that's happened tonight, and I shall identify you as a man who hit a policeman.'

'You wouldn't do a thing like that!'

'You play the fool for another five minutes, and see,' said Gratton grimly. 'You take far too much for granted—by God, you do!' he exploded. 'I ought to run you out of the house. Sit down.'

'Er—be consistent, old boy,' gasped Claude.

'Sit *down!*'

Claude sat down. 'Now let's get things right, old boy. *I'm* not the Boss. It's Dawlish who dishes out the orders—'

'He's not dishing out any orders to me,' said Gratton.

'Well, let's call 'em requests. I mean—'

'Listen to me,' said Gratton fiercely. 'I know nothing about this business except what's happened today. I have no interest in Dawlish, Fryer or Judy Bell. There's no reason in the world why I should help any of you. It's a murderous business and it ought to be handled by the police. It's bad enough allowing a thing like this to happen, but when it comes to coolly making my flat your headquarters, ordering me about, and acting like a lunatic—it won't do.'

'Well, yes,' said Claude. 'I see what you mean. It must be a sobering sight to see us from the outside, as it were. As a bunch we *are* rather ingrown. I mean, an acquired taste. But I do assure you that we mean well, and are quite convinced that if the police are called in, Judy will be bumped off.'

'You couldn't have thought that when she telephoned to meet Dawlish at the club-house.'

'Well, we weren't sure. Could have been a trick. Don't let's make any mistake about this, Gratton. Judy's in a very nasty spot. And if it lightens your doubts in any way as to our integrity, Dawlish's credentials are all very top drawer. Best friends with Superintendent Trivett of the Yard, and cousin or something or other of the Assistant Commissioner, and a devoted fruit farmer.'

'Then he shouldn't behave like a third-form schoolboy,' said Gratton loudly and fiercely. 'The mess he's involved me in is *most* irregular.'

'But of *course*. That's the whole point of it, I've been helping him on and off for years, and it always happens. And—seriously—he wouldn't ask you to go with us unless he felt pretty sure you were all right. It isn't easy to get listed among Dawlish's reliables. Sometimes takes years. Of course, he's been checking up on you. He knows you've a fortnight's holiday, starting now, that you're footloose and fancy free and can keep your head in a tight corner. When you work it out, old chap, he's shown considerable faith in you. It's really an honour.'

'It's an honour I can well do without,' said Gratton, but his voice was quieter, and considerably less fierce.

'But just think,' urged Claude, 'what would have happened if he'd considered you unworthy. Why, you'd still be playing bat and ball!'

Gratton drew in a deep breath and burst out laughing.

Claude gave a sigh of relief.

'That's all right then. Now I think we ought to get forty winks if we're to be off early in the morning.'

*   *   *

Freddie showed no signs of coming round, and they took him into the spare room, piled blankets over him and, at Claude's suggestion put a hot-water bottle near his feet. Claude was to use the other bed in that room, and Gratton retired to his own, not sure whether he was an utter fool or not.

He woke up just after seven o'clock, to see Claude standing by his bedside with a cup of tea.

Gratton struggled up, feeling at a considerable disadvantage. 'Thanks. Freddie awake?'

'Awake, but decidedly glum. Says he doesn't mind whether we take him with us or bury him. One good thing, he doesn't want any breakfast. We've a crust left, haven't we?'

'Hardly,' said Gratton.

'Hmm. Tell you what, let's get off early and have something on the road.'

'All right,' said Gratton, trying to keep his voice sternly non-committal, for he was conscious now, of a certain eagerness at the prospect of the adventures before them.

They left at half-past eight.

The village of Merrance nestled between hills which dropped sheer into the sea some thirty miles from Land's End. It was late in the afternoon when the two cars breasted a hill from which they could see the village and the River Mer. They had driven without a stop from Exeter, Claude and Freddie in one car, Gratton in the other, and it was now five o'clock.

The sun, sinking low, sent a vivid light over the valley, shining through the hills and striking the tops of the houses down below. Beyond the village was a sandy foreshore, running down to a small cove. It was less than a mile away; and they could see easily enough, the jagged rocks, sharp and cruel which lay at the foot of the cliffs.

'Quite a spot. I hope there's a good pub,' remarked Freddie.

'The A.A. book gives the *Lobster Pot* three stars,' said Claude hopefully. 'I wonder if that could be Tor House?'

He pointed towards a distant hill, which lay north of the village, near the top of which a house stood stark and grey, a large, forbidding place, deeply shadowed. The only road led from the village, and seemed no more than a track.

'Cheerful chap, aren't you?' remarked Freddie. 'Well, shall we get a move on?'

Gratton threw off the momentary depression caused by the appearance of the house on the hill. There was nothing to suggest that it was Tor House; Claude had been guessing.

'See you at the *Lobster Pot*,' called Claude. 'Don't stay mooning there too long.'

Gratton grinned, and waved to them. He was reluctant to leave this spot. The view was perfect, and the spell of the village lay over him. He watched the Austin until it disappeared round a curve in the road. A small bridge spanned the river, built of light grey stone. Two men were walking across it. He narrowed his eyes and stared more intently. The couple stopped on the middle of the bridge and leaned over the parapet, looking towards the bleak house on the hillside.

Gratton turned back to his car, and was opening the door when he heard stones falling. Turning abruptly, he saw an elderly, weather-beaten man climbing over the wall. The newcomer was dressed in a rough, tweed suit, and carried a stick. He made a picturesque sight against the deepening blue sky.

'Day to you, sir,' he greeted. 'Lovely weather.'

'Perfect.'

'Aye. Visiting these parts?'

'Just for a short holiday,' said Gratton.

The other nodded and smiled and began to walk down the road.

The brief encounter heightened the spell of the place for Gratton. He went downhill in third, glancing right and left. The two tall men still leaned against the parapet; it might be imagination that they were watching the house on the hill.

They had gone when he passed the end of the bridge.

Gratton made his way to the *Lobster Pot*.

Two cars were standing in the yard, but—Claude's Austin wasn't one of them.

Gratton frowned. Surely they would have come straight here? As he walked into the wide entrance hall he saw again the two men who had been on the bridge.

An oldish man sat behind the reception desk. He looked up.

'Good-evening, sir.'

'Good-evening,' said Gratton. 'I think my friends have already booked for me.'

'Have they, sir? What name would they have booked under, please?' The receptionist glanced at the register, which lay open in front of him.

'Gratton,' said Gratton.

'And how long ago would they have reserved a room, sir?'

'Only half an hour,' said Gratton.

The man shook his head gently.

'There must be some mistake, sir, we haven't had anyone here during the last half hour—no one at all, sir.'

Gratton watched the porter unfasten his suit-case from the back of the car, signed the register, was given Room 11, and followed the porter upstairs. He stood in the middle of a large double room as the door closed. It was like Claude to go off on some wild errand. There was really no reason to feel worried, and yet—

Someone tapped on the door.

'Come in,' called Gratton, startled.

The door opened, and the larger of the two men who had been sitting downstairs came in.

Genial and smiling, the flash of his white teeth redeemed a pleasant, but unnotable face.

'Hallo,' he said. 'Where are the others? You did all come together, didn't you?'

CHAPTER TEN

CAUSE FOR ALARM

Gratton said quietly: 'Who are you?'

'Ted Beresford,' said the other promptly. 'Don't say you weren't warned about us.'

'Tim and Ted,' said Gratton. He sat down heavily on the luggage stool. 'Oh, yes I was warned about you.'

'Go on. Well?'

'The main point stressed was that we shouldn't be seen together.'

'We've rooms on this floor, and I haven't advertised the face that I've nipped in to see you. You don't look too happy. Any trouble?'

'You know as much as I do,' answered Gratton. 'Freddie and Claude came ahead of me—less than half an hour ago. I stayed at the top of the hill for ten minutes.'

'Just to see the view?'

'Well, it's worth seeing, isn't it?' said Gratton defensively. It didn't matter what the situation, Dawlish and his friends always seemed to have him at a disadvantage. 'Nothing *could* have happened to them. They obviously took the wrong turning.'

'There is only one road from that hill,' said Beresford. 'I saw the two cars. Did you meet anyone up there?'

'No—well, I saw a fellow who looked like a shepherd.'

'Oh,' said Beresford abruptly. His smile faded. 'Medium build, well-worn tweeds, carrying a stick?'

Gratton felt his anxiety increasing.

'Yes, that's right.'

'Did he stay with you long?'

'No, only a few minutes. Look here—'

'That chap took an inordinate interest in Ted and me,' said Beresford grimly. 'Rather more than customary in a fellow who is supposed to be a hermit.' He pushed his hand through his thick curly hair. 'Well, it's no use worrying, but I wish they'd turn up.'

Gratton said irritably: 'How did you get here so early in the morning? According to Claude, you were near the copse last night.'

'We flew,' said Beresford simply.

'*Flew!*'

'There are aeroplanes,' said Beresford. 'Pat hasn't arrived yet, nor has Fryer, although I think Judy's here.'

'In—in the hotel?'

'No, at Tor House. I've gathered from the natives that a car arrived there early this morning with a girl passenger. Might not be Judy, of course, but it seems probable. Question is, what to do?'

'*I* don't know,' said Gratton.

'Obviously not. Better give the others half an hour,' said Beresford. 'We're in rooms 5 and 6. Good view of Tor House,' he added. 'Want to know when Fryer arrives.' He moved to the door. 'If you want us, give three taps with a pause after the first two. And don't leave the *Lobster Pot* without letting us know, will you?'

Gratton nodded agreement to both these injunctions. He was about to say, surely this game of cops and robbers had gone on long enough? But the door had closed.

He decided not to unpack. The likely thing was that Freddie and Claude had gone to another hotel. He wished now that he had not agreed to stay at the *Lobster Pot*, but he had more or less, by implication, given his word. There could be no harm, however, in going downstairs.

He passed the receptionist who smiled brightly, and went outside. A few people were sitting about at rustic tables.

Gratton ordered a pint of the local brew and sat down.

Every time he heard a car, he waited tensely, in the hope that it would be Claude and Freddie.

Hope rose again at the sound of an oncoming engine. It was a Rolls Royce, going towards the bridge. A chauffeur was at the wheel, and its one passenger was a woman—

Gratton started so violently that he nearly dropped his tankard; for the passenger was Judy Bell!

The car disappeared with surprising speed along the road which led to Tor House.

He stood watching. Then became conscious that someone was watching him. It was the hermit.

He would have rushed with his news to Room 5, but now he loitered deliberately, imagining eyes looking at him from the most unlikely corners. He reached it finally, and gave the arranged signal. Tap. Tap. Pause. Tap.

The door opened immediately, and he slipped inside, keeping his voice as low, and cool, as possible.

'Did you see that Rolls?'

Beresford smiled indulgently. 'Oh, yes. It belongs to Reddelow. Owner of Tor House. What are you looking so worked up about?'

'Judy was in that car!'

Beresford said slowly: 'Was she, then! Hear that, Tim?'

For the first time Gratton had a close-up of his companion. Like Beresford, he was dressed in a sports jacket and grey flannels; and like Beresford, he had a lazy, almost casual air with him.

'Are you sure?'

'I couldn't mistake her.'

Tim thrust his hands deep into his pockets, eyeing Gratton narrowly.

'The hermit was at the bridge,' added Gratton self-consciously.

'Quick of you to spot the blighter,' remarked Beresford. 'Tried the local brew yet? Good stuff! We keep a little in reserve,' he added, taking a bottle from the side of the bed, 'and an odd tankard for guests.' Gravely, he poured out beer.

There was something similar about all these people; Dawlish, Claude, Tim, and Ted all had an undefinable 'something'. It was partly confidence, partly calmness. Their facetiousness should have seemed out of place, but somehow it seemed characteristic and right. Gratton took the beer, feeling that whatever else, he was with men who knew what they were doing; good men in a crisis; the type who had performed great deeds during the war.

Beresford walked to the window, and Gratton noticed that he had a limp.

'What are we going to do?' he asked.

'Only thing we can. I fancy that Freddie and Claude saw something they thought worth following and chased after it, though it's odd that we didn't see them come into the village. There's only one small road leading from that hill,' he added, 'it's a dead-end, leading to the sea.'

'I should think we ought to have a look at it,' suggested Gratton.

'Could do.' Timothy hesitated, then took a penny from his

pocket and spun it into the air. He caught it and slapped it on to the back of his left hand, keeping it covered.

'Heads,' said Beresford.

Jeremy removed his hand.

'Tails,' he said. 'Bad luck, Ted! All right, Gratton, you and I will go and have a look at that sea road. Ted will stay here, watch the house and take any messages there may be.'

Gratton said nothing; the little by-play with the penny was also characteristic of these men.

When they were in the car, and Gratton started off, Tim Jeremy said:

'We're as much in the dark as you are. All we know is that Fryer said he was coming down here, and that the girl was on the way. You know, of course, that she's in a spot?'

'Oh, yes, I know that,' said Gratton.

'It's a murky business, whichever way you look at it,' declared Tim Jeremy. 'We've taken part in quite a few shows, one way and the other, but there's something about this one that I don't like. The fact that Fryer's always held his hand at the last minute— never really committed murder—makes it worse. I'm beginning to have my doubts about the wisdom of keeping the police out of it.'

'I'm glad someone has a glimmering of sense,' retorted Gratton.

'One wants considerably more than a glimmering to deal with Fryer,' Jeremy assured him. 'Getting darkish. isn't it? Better put on the headlights, we don't want to miss the turning.'

Bright lights suddenly pierced the gloom making the night beyond its beam seem darker. Gratton watched the right-hand side carefully, for it was on that side that the sea lay. Suddenly, a sign post, lurching forward drunkenly, appeared in the glow.

Gratton slowed down, and could just read the sign: *River*

Caves. He swung the car into the narrow road which rose steeply. On the left, the overhanging branches of a tall hedge scraped lingeringly against the side of the car.

At last they reached the top.

The last magic light of afterglow spread over the sea, and out of it the rocks and cliffs rose, dark, phantom shapes, silent, sinister. A gentle murmur of the waves washing the shore was the only sound now that the engine was silent.

Both men felt the dark mystery of the place.

'There isn't any sign of their car,' Gratton said at last, striving to keep casual. 'Not much chance of seeing traces of a flinty road like this. Shall we drive on?'

Jeremy grinned at him.

'Try it and see,' he said; but when Gratton re-started the car, Jeremy grabbed his arm. 'I was only fooling, you ass!'

'You fool too much,' said Gratton sourly. 'What's the matter?'

They got out of the car and with Jeremy leading, they walked forward. Suddenly Gratton found himself on the edge of the cliff. Only a steep path led downwards, dark, gloomy, and dangerous.

Gratton felt shaken.

'If I hadn't stopped when I had—'

'No need to give ourselves the heebie-jeebies,' said Jeremy. 'I thought you knew that was the end of the cliff. Haven't you studied a map of the district?'

'No.'

Jeremy said comfortably: 'I've got a good survey map here,' he touched his pocket. 'This path leads down to the River Caves. Unless it's dried up for the summer, there's an underground river which spills out into the sea. If Freddie and Claude came down here and disappeared, then—'

Gratton said in a strained voice: 'They might have driven straight over the top!'

'Well, let's take the bright view,' said Jeremy. 'No reason to think that Fryer's ready for the slaughter, yet.'

'It would look like an accident.'

'Hmm, yes,' said Jeremy. 'Well, we'll see. According to this map,' he went on, tapping his pocket again, 'there are two ways down. This one, which is called Neck-breaker Path—attractive name, isn't it?—and another one, on the right here, which isn't so steep. Have you a torch?'

'There's one in the dashboard pocket.'

'Better get it,' said Jeremy. 'I've got one, but I'm never too sure of the batteries.'

Gratton went back for the torch, flicking it on, to see if it was working. As he did so, he caught the flicker of movement.

A man had appeared in the light, only to vanish. Tight-lipped, Gratton hurried back to Jeremy.

'Did you see him?' he demanded.

'See him? See *what*?' asked Jeremy. 'Are you sure it wasn't a sheep?' He looked quickly at Gratton's stony face, he added appeasingly, 'Er—you don't happen to carry a gun, do you?'

'Of course I don't.'

'All right,' said Jeremy. 'I'll do the shooting.'

He led the way down the path, which was well-defined for the first hundred yards, twisting through rocks and boulders and the coarse undergrowth which grew out of the face of the cliff. After the first five minutes, it became steeper.

Jeremy had gone far ahead, and Gratton could only just see the glow of his torch. He called: 'Wait a minute!' and Jeremy's answer floated back, as if from a long way off. But the sound of movement of displaced stones, stopped. Gratton took out his torch and switched it on. The beam shone on a gap almost immediately in front of him; a false step, and he would have fallen hundreds of feet to the rocks below.

Soberly, step by step, he made his way between the boulders. It seemed to take a long time. Surely he should have caught up with Jeremy? And then he saw that Jeremy's light was out.

'Ahoy there!' he called.

Only the echoes answered him.

'*Ahoy there!*' His voice grew strident, for his throat was suddenly dry. '*Ahoy there, Jeremy!*'

The echo, merging with the roar of the sea, came back to him; but there was no other sound. And now it was almost dark. The stars were bright; but they shed no light, certainly not enough for him to see by.

'*Jeremy! Are you there?*'

'*Are—you—there?*' came the echo.

He stood quite still, shining his torch about him, cold, frightened. The roaring waves seemed to be much louder now; as if they were calling to him. He took a step forward, and kicked against something which gave out a metallic ring. Swiftly, he turned the torch downward.

He had kicked against another torch; Jeremy's.

CHAPTER ELEVEN

DARK MYSTERY

Gratton picked up the torch with cold fingers. Jeremy must have been attacked, abducted; he couldn't have—he simply *couldn't* have fallen down the cliff, had he done so he would have shouted out, screamed, shattered the quiet of the night because he would have known that he was falling to certain death.

Silence—darkness—mystery.

Could Jeremy have slipped?

Gratton held his breath and stepped forward, shining his torch until suddenly the earth seemed to vanish. Now he knew that he was standing at the edge of the cliff, and Jeremy had only been a few feet from here.

Something wet and cold fell on Gratton's face; spray.

Jeremy had said something about an underground river which flowed into the sea near River Caves. Gratton backed away from the edge, trying to decide what to do. If only there were more light! He played the beam of his torch slowly, examining every spot—

Something moved!

A hand—he saw it clearly, a hand gripping a rock not twenty feet in front of him!

Gratton crept forward, his heart banging against his ribs. Yes, there it was again! He watched, hardly daring to breathe.

Another hand appeared; and then a man's head, rearing up as if from the bowels of the earth.

If only he dared shine the torch on the man.

Why not? The advantage was surely with him.

Whoever it was was now out of the hole, and upright; he seemed enormous.

Gratton flashed the torch into the man's face—then stood petrified, hardly able to believe his eyes.

It was Dawlish!

'Ted—'

'It's—Gratton,' called Gratton.

A whisper came back to him. 'Come over here—slowly, as if you're still looking for the path.'

Gratton obeyed.

'You aren't alone, are you?'

'I wasn't,' said Gratton.

'Who came with you? Tim or Ted?'

'Jeremy.'

'Tim, eh? What happened to him?'

'He just—just disappeared.'

'Whereabouts?'

'Somewhere from this ledge. Didn't you see anything?'

'I've only just come up for air,' said Dawlish. 'It's quite a spot down there. Caverns,' he added, 'a series of them and they're built on top of one another. Quite fantastic rock formation, too, almost as good as Cheddar. Ted at the *Lobster Pot*?'

'Yes. But Freddie and Claude—'

Gratton found himself telling the story in swift, graphic sentences. Dawlish listened to him without interrupting, until he mentioned seeing Judy Bell in the Rolls Royce. And then Dawlish emitted a low-pitched whistle.

'So Reddelow's in it,' he commented. 'Toby, I think we're getting somewhere.'

'Oh, do you,' growled Gratton. 'We started off seven strong and now there are three of us, we haven't helped Judy Bell, and it would take one push to send you and me down on those rocks—then there'd be only one,' he added sourly. 'We're getting somewhere all right; into a hell of a mess.'

Dawlish grunted.

'Not as bad as all that, surely. Here we are standing on top of one of the neatest rock formations in Cornwall, with caves which run the dickens of a long way under the hills, possibly as far as Tor House. Which is Reddelow's house,' he added. 'I didn't know that until a couple of hours ago, and as Judy's been seen in his Rolls, we can assume that he's in it. And that explains a lot.'

'Who *is* Reddelow?' snapped Gratton peevishly.

'A recently retired under secretary at the Home Office,' said Dawlish, 'a man who resigned ostensibly because he'd reached retiring age, actually because there was some scandal which I fancy was hushed up. Men in high places are concerned quite a bit in this affair, old chap, that's one reason why we have to be very cautious indeed. But we've a whale of a job on.'

'At least you admit that,' said Gratton.

'No point in blinking at facts,' said Dawlish. 'And the most significant ones are that Freddie and Claude disappeared near here and that Tim was only thirty or forty yards in front of you when *he* disappeared. Undoubtedly he's somewhere in the caves. We'll wait another ten minutes and then investigate.'

The waiting would have been nerve wracking, if Dawlish had

not begun to talk quietly and fluently. They seemed to be utterly alone on the cliffside. Yet so completely was Gratton under the big man's spell that he did not think—as he would have done with Claude or any of the others—of saying that they were wasting time, and allowing Tim Jeremy to be taken further and further away.

Dawlish's story absorbed him, for he had deliberately walked into an expected trap, leaving Claude, Tim and Ted outside, without telling Gratton or Freddie they were there. That, he admitted freely, was because he was afraid that they might crack under interrogation, and he did not want Fryer to know the truth, although undoubtedly the fat man suspected it.

After he had gone into the 'torture chamber' Fryer had threatened and blustered, trying to frighten him into giving up his interest in Judy Bell. Then, after half an hour or so, one of the guards had come in to report that two policemen were in the grounds, and, from their conversation, it appeared that others were on the way. It transpired that Fryer had been using the bungalow, which was at one time a private museum, for the past two months. According to the conversation overheard by the man in the grounds, the owner of the house had suspected that the bungalow was being used for illegal purposes and had asked the police to keep an eye on it. That night, several men had been seen approaching, and a warning had immediately been sent to the police.

At the first suspicion of this, Fryer had decamped, taking Dawlish with him.

Dawlish, travelling in the last of four cars, had waited until they were on the outskirts of Oxford, and then overpowered his driver and taken control of the car! Thus, he had been able to follow Fryer to his Oxford Hotel. He had been lucky enough to overhear a significant sentence or two mentioning Tor House.

Immediately Tim and Ted had arrived he had told them to hire a private aeroplane and fly to Cornwall, so that they could watch the house before Fryer arrived.

'And you? Did you fly here too?' asked Gratton.

'Oh, no,' Dawlish said disarmingly. 'I came in the old bus. I was waiting near the hedge on the main road when Fryer and his mob—four men in all—reached here. I thought they would go straight to Tor House. Instead, they took the low road. So I cut across here, taking the route you used, and climbed down the cliff. And that's where I came unstuck,' he added, with a ghost of a grin. 'There was a motor-boat waiting, inside a cave, and Fryer and his men made off in that. The move dished me completely. But I thought it worth looking round, and while doing so discovered the caves. It wouldn't surprise me if we aren't in the middle of a smuggling racket, but it's too early to jump to conclusions. Of course, Fryer went to Tor House,' he added.

'By sea?'

'Yes. The house has its own landing stage. Fryer must have suspected that the road was being watched. But now I think it's time we got a move on.'

'Aren't we too late?' asked Gratton, privately thinking that Dawlish had talked far too long, and all hope was lost of catching up with Jeremy.

'Oh, I don't think so,' said Dawlish. 'If we'd followed too close on their heels, they'd have heard us—sounds travel a long way in those caves.'

'But they may not have left any traces.'

Dawlish laughed outright.

'Tim knew there was a risk of something going wrong, and tipped his heels with luminous paint. It'll leave traces for two or three nights. He's been in shows like this before.'

'Oh,' said Gratton.

'So let's get cracking,' said Dawlish.

He led the way forward.

It was no longer necessary to use a torch. The moonlight was already shining on the small smears of luminous paint. There were several about the spot where Gratton had found the torch, and it was easy to reconstruct what had happened; someone had struck Jeremy down when he had been looking for the path, and either carried, or dragged, him off.

'One thing's certain,' whispered Dawlish, 'they didn't use the hole I came up by, so there must be another quite near.'

Gratton grunted.

Their task was made easier because the smears disappeared completely just beyond the place where the torch had been lying. Therefore, they concentrated their search within a narrow radius of that point.

Gratton put out a hand to steady himself against a boulder— and the boulder swayed under his weight.

Cautiously, experimentally, they pushed from every point. Suddenly, with a startling ease, the boulder rolled a couple of feet, disclosing a dark void.

'Looks promising,' said Dawlish. 'I'm going to use the torch.'

He flashed it on, keeping his fingers closed over the bulb, so that only a faint glimmer of light showed. It was enough to reveal the hole, about a foot wide and a yard long, over which the boulder had been placed. Dawlish peered down from one side, Gratton from the other. Dawlish took a finger from the front of the torch and shone the beam downwards. It revealed a roughly cut step, and on it could be seen a faint, luminous smear.

'That's more like it,' said Dawlish with a satisfied grin. 'I'm going down. Follow as soon as I call, and for God's sake don't flash the torch on to the cliffs.'

He lowered himself into the hole. The first step was about five feet down. Soon he disappeared completely.

Again Gratton waited in the silence of the night, the background of the waterfall seeming to heighten the silence.

Time seemed interminable.

Now that he was alone, Gratton could imagine men waiting down those steps, prepared to attack Dawlish before the big man had a chance to defend himself.

Gratton peered upwards.

The headlights of his car were still visible, a good two or three hundred feet above him. How far he had come!

Suddenly a hollow whisper wafted up from the depth of the hole. 'O.K. Toby!'

Gratton took a last look at the gaunt cliffs, before stepping over the edge, and groped for the top step.

As he touched it, the lights on his car went out!

CHAPTER TWELVE

UNDERGROUND

'Come on!' whispered Dawlish.

Gratton, staring into the darkness, knew that there was nothing else to do, he must get down and tell Dawlish what had happened. The going was easier than he had expected, and by holding on to the walls he was able to walk down the steps, backwards. Suddenly he heard Dawlish's voice close behind him.

'That's the last step. We're in the top cave.'

Dawlish had tied a handkerchief round his torch. Its dimmed light was quite enough to show them a wide passage, occasionally smeared with tiny flecks of luminous paint.

Dawlish said: 'The tunnel slopes down, and it's fairly dry and easy going. I went as far as another flight of steps.'

'Dawlish,' said Gratton solemnly.

'Hm-hm?'

'Someone's switched off my headlights. Just now. I saw them go out.'

'Have they, be'gad!' exclaimed Dawlish. 'You're sure? The battery hasn't failed?'

'It was charged at the week-end,' said Gratton.

'Hm. Well, we always knew there was a risk of being seen,' said Dawlish philosophically. 'No use worrying too much. We've got to take things as they come.'

Dawlish handed him the torch.

It was evident that they were walking along a natural tunnel. Sometimes it was wide enough for three men to walk abreast, at others it was only just wide enough for one. Now the ceiling was several feet above his head, next moment so low that he had to duck. Suddenly the dim light shone upon a step.

Gratton started down, counting in a whisper.

'One . . . two . . . three . . . four . . . five . . .' There seemed no end to them.

'. . . fifteen . . . sixteen.'

Ah! There was the last step, and a passage, which appeared to slope downwards.

'Nineteen,' he said as he reached the bottom and stood waiting for Dawlish to join him. The roof here was very low. If anyone were to spring out at them they would have little chance to defend themselves.

There were odd little noises, too—creaks and groans, which played on his nerves; but there was one good thing. The pale smears which showed where Jeremy had been, still stretched along the passage.

As the cave widened, the whispering and creaking became louder. There were deep caverns of darkness on either side, too far for the torch to reach. The waterfall must be very near, thought Gratton.

He stopped.

'We ought to take the handkerchief off the torch,' he said, 'we can see what we're doing better.'

'All right,' agreed Dawlish. 'Although Tim—'

Across his words came a sharp report! A *crack*! which

sounded very loud, then echoed in weird medley. *Crack-ack-ack-ack-ack!* Even Dawlish jumped, and Gratton could hear his own heart thumping.

They stood quite still.

Crack!

As the echoes clattered about them, whispering up in the roof and round the walls, Dawlish put a steadying hand on Gratton's shoulder.

'That's shooting,' he said.

'Yes,' agreed Gratton, his mouth dry. 'Jeremy had a gun.'

'He wouldn't use it unless—'

Crack! Ack-ack-ach-ack-ack!

'Can't tell how far it is away,' said Dawlish. 'Sound is pretty deceptive in a cave. Let's get on a bit.'

He pushed forward, half a step ahead. A few yards further on another shot sounded, the loudest they had yet heard—and Gratton saw a faint flash.

'Getting warm,' said Dawlish. 'Put the light out.'

Gratton obeyed.

For a moment they stood in utter darkness; but soon that was broken by a flash followed almost at once by the roar of a shot—three shots this time, in quick succession.

'They're shooting it out,' said Dawlish.

They crept forward, passing from one cave to another. Groping forward torch in hand, Gratton hardly dared to breathe.

Crack! Ack-ack-ack-ack!

'Down,' whispered Dawlish.

They dropped to their hands and knees, crawling along for a few yards, before the silence and blackness which had closed about them was rent by another burst of shooting in which every part of the cavern was illuminated.

The whole picture lay before them.

Men were crouching behind rocks at one side of the cavern, shooting towards the other, from which the return fire was coming.

Dawlish whispered.

'Get close to the wall. Better let me get in front,' he added, and crawled past.

Gratton saw the gun in his hand. He had recognised, too, one of the men behind the rocks; it was Karloff.

If Karloff and his companions glanced round, they would see Dawlish. As Gratton crawled behind the big man, he wondered what form of attack Dawlish would make.

The wall of the cave curved inwards.

After two breathless minutes, Dawlish passed behind a rock; even a glance during the shooting would not reveal him. He did not speak again; they were too near Karloff, and whispers would travel clearly, but Gratton divined his intention; he wanted to get near enough to attack without shooting.

Prisoners would talk . . .

He was no more than ten yards from Karloff. But to reach him, he would have to forsake cover. Gratton could now see Jeremy, Claude, and Freddie, and that there was no way of escape for them, without dashing for it.

Another burst of shooting; *crack-ack-ack-ack-ack*. Karloff's men firing three shots to Jeremy's one.

Dawlish still crawled forward.

Now Gratton was sure that Dawlish intended to get *behind* Karloff. The gap between Karloff and his men was only a couple of yards, but their attention was riveted on the group opposite. It took a cool nerve, but Dawlish didn't hesitate and Gratton followed him unquestioningly.

Suddenly, as Karloff loosed off another shot, it occurred to Gratton that he and Dawlish were in the line of Jeremy's fire.

Jeremy didn't shoot.

Had he seen them? Or had he run out of ammunition?

Dawlish was now only three yards from his objective.

There was a lull in the shooting.

Into the silence came Karloff's voice.

'You had enough over there?'

No one answered.

'You can't get away,' Karloff said, 'and you're out of ammunition. Better give up.'

Again there was no answer.

'I've warned you,' Karloff said. 'If you shoot again—'

'My dear chap,' said Dawlish, 'how can they shoot again if they've run out of ammunition? Don't move!'

Karloff said in a cracked voice:

'Dawlish—'

'Keep still,' snapped Dawlish. 'Tim, come and take their guns. I—'

Karloff raised his gun as Dawlish spoke. Two shots rang out in quick succession. Karloff gasped and dropped his gun, which clattered to the floor, while his own bullet smacked into the wall behind Dawlish's head.

'That's enough,' Dawlish said.

Tim crossed the cavern in a few long strides, and the other two men let him take their guns without making the slightest attempt to fight. Karloff, holding his right arm to his chest, stared malignantly at Dawlish.

'Dear old boy!' called Claude jubilantly. 'You haven't brought any beer with you, I suppose?'

'Not this trip,' said Dawlish. 'Why don't you come over here?'

'Can't,' said Claude. 'Hamstrung. That is, my wrists and ankles are tied, and poor old Freddie had a fall and his right ankle's about the size of an elephant's—but he's very much alive.'

Karloff snapped: 'He won't be for long, you—'

'Hush,' said Dawlish. 'You've had your day, little man. Anywhere handy we can park 'em, Tim?'

'Just the place,' Jeremy said, 'there's a small cave behind us, and we can roll a rock in front of the entrance. They'll be as safe as if they were in a prison cell. March, gents,' he ordered, and stuck his gun into one man's ribs.

Half an hour later, in the light of the torch, Dawlish, Gratton and the others sat on small boulders and assessed the situation.

Freddie was worse off than any of the party. His ankle was in a bad way, and he had wrenched his right shoulder. Claude had come off comparatively lightly and Tim was battered but workable.

First Claude, then Jeremy, had told their stories.

Soon after leaving the brow of the hill, Claude had seen Judy Bell going towards River Caves! Without pausing to think, Claude had swung the car off the road, and gone after her. By the time Claude reached the top of the cliff, she had disappeared.

'We nearly had it, old pippin,' said Claude. 'Didn't know we'd reached a precipice. Just saw the drop in time. Jammed on the old brakes as a couple of tykes jumped from the side of the cliff and dotted us. I went right out, but Freddie managed to put up a fight. You see the result. Neither of us remember anything that happened after that, but we woke up to find ourselves where Karloff is now. And soon afterwards, they brought Tim in. Your turn, Tim.'

Tim Jeremy, searching for a safe path, had been completely surprised by a man dropping a cloth over his head. With a gun in his ribs, and unable to see, he had been pushed down the hole and eventually landed up in Karloff's cave.

'They were in a frightful hurry,' he added. 'Made a purely

nominal job of tying me up—expecting, I suppose, to come back later and do the thing in style—and forgot to take my gun. We were crawling towards the entrance when they came in again, and started shooting.'

Dawlish said thoughtfully: 'I think they're getting the wind up. Question is, should we go forward or go back? If we were all able-bodied, I wouldn't ask, but Freddie's got to have that leg seen to. He won't be able to climb up the cliff on his own, so he'll need someone with him—two people for preference.'

'Let's toss for it,' suggested Jeremy. He dipped his hand into his pocket, and took out a handful of coins. Gravely, he handed Dawlish, Claude, and Gratton one apiece. 'First odd man out stays. Second odd man out stays. Afterwards heads or tail—we can only spare one man to go into the village with Freddie,' he added.

Four coins went into the air, were slapped down on the backs of four hands and, after a moment's pause, all were uncovered.

Dawlish was heads; all the others were tails.

They tossed again; Claude was odd man out.

'Between you and me for the last place,' said Tim.

'Heads,' interrupted Gratton.

Jeremy grinned and tossed. 'Tails,' he said. 'Sorry, old boy.'

'Now we've got that sorted out,' said Dawlish, 'you go with Gratton and Freddie to the hole in the cliff, and keep them covered until they reach the top, Tim. There was someone about, and they might run into trouble. See them safely off in the car, and then come back here. Claude and I will have a little session with Karloff—'

'You'll never move that boulder!' exclaimed Tim.

'Won't I?' asked Dawlish.

It was a long, eerie journey back to the hole, and even worse when they were on the cliff. Freddie was in acute pain all the time, but apart from an occasional gasp, he made no complaint. Gratton was afraid every moment that there would be an attack on them, but they reached the car safely. The lights were still out, but the car appeared to be in order, the engine turned at the first touch of the self-starter.

They left Tim standing and watching them.

The journey to the *Lobster Pot* was uneventful.

The porter helped Gratton to carry Freddie upstairs and within twenty minutes a doctor had arrived, examined the ankle, pulled a wry face and said that the ankle should be X-rayed, and he would be much better off in the local nursing home for the night.

It was nearly nine o'clock before Gratton returned from the nursing home, confident that Freddie was well-looked after, but feeling strangely forlorn at being on his own.

After a lonely dinner Gratton went upstairs and tapped on the doors of Rooms 5 and 6, but no one was there— where *had* Beresford gone?

He decided to use the single room for himself, after all. It was pleasant enough. He strolled to the window and looked out, into a starry moonlight night, wishing he could see Tor House. On the spur of the moment, he crossed the passage and entered Beresford's room.

Lights were shining from several windows of the house on the Tor.

He watched them for ten minutes; nothing happened, nothing moved. He lit a cigarette and went back to his own room. Opening the door he stepped inside, putting on the light.

Judy Bell blinked up at him from the bed!

CHAPTER THIRTEEN

JUDY BELL

She lay back on the bed, her legs curled up beneath her, her dark hair falling untidily. She wore a grey suit with a white blouse and some frilly lace at the neck and sleeves. Her shoes were on the floor at the side of the bed, one upright, the other on its side.

Gratton stood transfixed, his hand still on the electric switch.

'Hallo,' said Judy Bell, in a small voice.

Gratton drew a deep breath, stepped forward and then, as an afterthought, went back and locked the door, slipping the key into his pocket.

He wanted to be angry, he *insisted* on being angry.

'You have a nerve,' he said heavily.

She sat up very straight and said childishly: 'As a matter of fact, I'm so frightened I hardly know what I'm doing.'

'You tried that one on Dawlish,' said Gratton, 'it's most unoriginal to attempt the same dodge twice.' He stared down at her; and no matter how he tried, he could not stifle the furious beating of his heart.

He *had* entered into this affair because of her; he hadn't fully realised it before, but now he knew that was true.

'But—things are different now. I thought Dawlish could help before, now I know that he can't, no one can.'

'You don't seem to need much,' said Gratton.

'No, I don't,' she said, and suddenly she leaned forward her hands clenched. 'That's why I've come here, what I want to tell you and Dawlish. Where *is* Dawlish?'

'Round about,' said Gratton.

'It's no use, you've all got to go,' said Judy, 'I thought we had a chance, now—' she swung her legs from the bed, and stood up. A strand of hair fell on to her cheek and she brushed it impatiently aside. 'Mr. Gratton, will you tell the others that? Tell them to leave Merrance *tonight.*'

'They won't leave Merrance tonight,' Gratton assured her. 'This has gone too far—'

'You must make them!'

'Don't be silly,' said Gratton sharply. He pulled a chair towards him and sat down. 'What's caused this change of heart?'

'I've told you.'

'You're frightened—but you've been saying that for some time. Three weeks or more, according to Dawlish.'

'It's much worse now,' she said, '*much* worse.'

Unless she was a superlative actress, she was terrified. He could see it in her eyes, in the way her lips were tensed, in the rigidity of her slim body. And she was tired; he hadn't noticed that before, but he could see it now; that was why she had rested on the bed.

Gratton felt himself weakening.

'You're talking nonsense!' he said harshly. 'Do you realise that men are risking their lives for you?'

She said quietly:

'That's why I've come. I didn't realise until this afternoon that these people will do murder to get what they want. And I'm afraid that if you—if Dawlish and his friends—try to help, they will be killed.'

Gratton could find nothing to say.

The girl moved forward, stretching out a hand to him. Gratton took it, filled with a sudden, inexplicable warmth.

'If I thought you could do anything, I wouldn't talk like this,' she went on, 'but I'm quite sure that they're too strong for you, and that it will only bring disaster if you go on with it. Surely you can persuade Dawlish that it's no use.'

'That's quite impossible,' Gratton declared roughly. He took his hand away and stood up. 'If you're in a spot, there isn't a better man than Dawlish to get you out of it.'

'But *no one* can get me out of this.'

'The police—' began Gratton.

'No!'she cried. 'No!'

The fear had lurked in her eyes before; now it showed like a naked flame.

'Why are you so scared of the police?' Gratton demanded, keeping his voice steady. 'This is a criminal business and they'll have to know sooner or later. Saying that you must avoid the police is like saying that you mustn't eat.'

The girl said abruptly:

'Mr. Gratton, I've been allowed an hour to talk to you. If I leave here without having your promise to persuade Dawlish to go away, I can't be responsible for what will happen but—I don't think you'll live another twenty-four hours. *Now* do you believe me?'

Yes, he believed her.

Yet even then the first shadow of doubt crossed his mind; and, once he perceived it, he marvelled that he had been unaware of it before. Supposing the girl herself had been frightened into taking some active part in whatever crimes were being perpetrated? Was there any proof that her life was in danger? She appeared to move about much as she liked; she might have come to the *Sola Club* expressly to lure Dawlish after her, to lead him into a trap.

'So your kind friends have allowed you one hour,' he said drily. 'What will happen if you don't get back on time?'

'I must.'

'Your mistake,' said Gratton, 'you're going to stay until Dawlish gets here, he can deal with you.' He tapped his pocket. 'The key's quite safe.'

'Don't be a fool!' she exclaimed.

'I've been a fool too often in this business, this time I'm taking no chances,' said Gratton.

'You must let me out,' said Judy desperately. 'You'll only increase your own danger if you try to keep me here.'

'According to you, that danger's already pretty acute,' retorted Gratton. 'Let's forget it, Judy Bell. You're here and you'll stay here until Dawlish comes. You may as well make up your mind to it. You may have the bed,' he added ironically, 'I'll take the easy chair. It's a pity you didn't go into the double room, we could have had a bed apiece then.'

She held out her hand.

'Give me the key.'

'Oh, no,' said Gratton.

'Oh, you *fool*!'

She turned away, as if she could not bear to let him see her face; and he thought there were tears in her eyes. He watched her open her bag and dab at her eyes with a small white hand-kerchief. No doubt—

She turned round, pointing a small automatic at him.

'Give me the key,' she said.

* * *

The gun was quite steady. Gratton believed that she would shoot if he delayed too long. He hardly knew whether to be furiously angry or to admire her calmness.

He had to make up his mind . . .

He put his hand to his pocket—*was* he going to give her the key? Was he going to allow a slip of a girl to escape from him twice, without making any attempt to make her stay or to disarm her?

He stepped forward, taking the key out of his pocket.

'Throw it to me!' she said urgently. 'Don't come any nearer!'

Gratton made as if to toss the key, then drew back his arm and flung it wide. In the fleeting second that her gaze followed its flight, he jumped at her, striking at the gun. He sent it flying from her fingers, and gripped her wrist. For a moment they stood locked together.

'You fool,' she gasped, 'this won't help you!'

'I've told you that you're going to stay until Dawlish comes,' said Gratton lightly, 'and that's the way it is.'

She kicked him violently on the shin, and the sharp point of her shoe sent a spasm of pain through his leg; but he maintained his hold. He could feel her breath on his cheeks, and see the fluttering of a pulse in her forehead.

'*You must let me go!*'

'You're only wasting your breath,' said Gratton, 'you're going to stay.'

But how? He glanced at the bed. If he made her get under the blankets, she wouldn't be able to get out without giving him plenty of warning.

He let her left wrist go, put his arm round her waist, and staggered to the bed.

'Get in there,' he said, 'and believe me, I've no personal designs—'

She screamed!

The move so startled him that he let her go. She watched him warily, backing to the door.

'Let me go,' she said quickly. 'If you don't, I'll scream again, the porter will come.' She glanced significantly at the rumpled bed. 'He'll think—'

Footsteps sounded in the passage, and a woman exclaimed:

'I'm sure it was on this floor!'

'*Open the door!*' hissed Judy, 'or I'll scream again!'

Gratton clenched his teeth, and muttered:

'All right, scream, damn you!'

She opened her lips—but no sound came. His gaze held hers, challenging, defying. If she did scream again it would be all up with him.

'I'm sure it was from this floor,' repeated the woman in the passage. 'Are you all right?' she called in a trembling voice. 'Is anything the matter?'

Someone tapped loudly on a door.

At the same time, the curtains moved at the window. Through the gap Gratton saw the muzzle of a gun. The man behind it was smiling. He had a weather-browned face, and his rough tweed coat was unmistakable. It was the hermit!

He climbed into the room. 'Now, little lady, hop out of the window, I'll deal with Mr. Gratton.'

She shot one quick glance at Gratton, then hurried to the window. As she disappeared, there was a loud tap on the door, and a man cried:

'Is anyone in there?'

The hermit picked up the key and tossed it to Gratton. If he were to avoid scandal, he would have to act quickly. He slipped the key into the lock, pretending to yawn as he pulled the door open.

'What—' he began, gazing in assumed surprise at the small crowd without. He yawned again. 'What on earth's the matter?'

'Did you hear a *scream*?' demanded one of the women.

'*Scream*?' echoed Gratton. 'No, I was dozing, and—'

'Let's try the next room!' someone snapped.

Gratton closed the door. The hermit stood just behind it; and his gun was no longer in sight.

'Sit down; young man,' he said, 'I want to talk to you.'

'And I wouldn't object to a chat with you,' said Gratton.

'Then we might be able to talk to our mutual advantage,' the hermit said quietly. 'Stop looking as if you would like to break my neck, and let's talk reasonably. The girl will be all right now—for a little while, at all events.'

CHAPTER FOURTEEN

THE 'HERMIT' SUGGESTS

The 'hermit' put a pipe to his mouth and struck a match, looking at Gratton as if he were more amused than angry. No sound came from the garden; Judy appeared to have escaped without being noticed. Gratton felt his anger cooling, there was no point in being difficult, and if the man had a suggestion to make it would be better to hear him out.

'You'd better sit down,' he said.

'Thanks.' The 'hermit' arranged himself comfortably on the end of the bed. 'I may as well say at once that I've a keen personal interest in Sir Henry Reddelow,' he began, 'and although we're not on friendly terms, I don't want him to come a cropper. At the moment he seems to be a cat's paw in the hands of certain unscrupulous rogues and I'm afraid he might be driven into doing something quite beyond the pale.'

Gratton made no comment.

'My name is Grey, by the way. George Grey. I learned your name from the register downstairs, and I gather that your friends Beresford and Jeremy, as well as the other two men whom you expected to find waiting for you here, aren't exactly well-disposed towards these unscrupulous rogues.'

'We are not,' said Gratton.

'Good! Mind you—' Grey took his pipe from his mouth and pointed the stem towards Gratton, 'if I hadn't heard the young woman talking to you, I wouldn't have been so sure of you. But since I am convinced that she was acting under orders in begging you to leave here, I'd rather you stayed. But I hope none of you will remain under any illusion about the toughness of the job you've taken on.'

'I think you can be assured of that,' said Gratton drily.

'Well, now we know where we are. There's Reddelow, Fryer's cat's paw—' there was the faintest pause after he mentioned Fryer's name, but Gratton showed no sign that it meant anything to him and Grey went on quietly: 'and Fryer is after something very big, and I fancy was getting away with it until the young woman came along. Just how and why she put a spoke in his wheel I don't know, but she did. And the spoke grew larger when she called on her friends. Well, that's summed up the parties concerned, I think, and—'

'You've been too modest,' said Gratton, 'you've forgotten to explain where you come in.'

'Just a friend of Reddelow's,' declared Grey, airily. 'I needn't go into details, but I don't want Reddelow to make a complete fool of himself. I think he's being blackmailed,' he added, 'but that's a pure speculation. How well do you know Fryer?'

'Well enough to want to see him hanged,' said Gratton.

'If there's a blacker rogue in the country I'll be surprised,' said Grey. 'And he has a pretty ruthless gang working for him.' He paused. 'At least one murder has been committed.'

Gratton drew in his breath.

'Ah,' said Grey, 'murder makes you think, doesn't it? A young man came down here a few days ago. Name of Paul.'

Into Gratton's mind there sprang the recollection of Dawlish, talking to him in the club-room. Dawlish believed that Paul was responsible for Judy Bell's disappearance and Gratton had assumed that Paul and Fryer were working together, but if he had been killed—but how could he take Grey's word for that, or for anything?

'He visited Reddelow and then left the house on foot,' said Grey. 'I followed him as he walked to the cliff behind Tor House. The cliff there is very steep, the drop to the rocks is nearly four hundred feet, and immediately below it is the whirlpool.'

He paused . . .

'And as he stood there, a man appeared from behind a rock and pushed him over,' Grey said starkly.

'Pushed—' echoed Gratton.

'There's no doubt about it,' Grey assured him. 'I saw it happen. I—I heard the scream.'

The room was silent; but the scream of a man plunging down to his doom seemed to echo in Gratton's ears.

'The body was picked up off Merrance Bay,' Grey continued soberly. 'The verdict at the inquest was accidental death.'

Gratton said slowly: 'You could have told the truth.'

'Oh, yes, I could have done that,' agreed Grey calmly, 'and yet—would I have been believed? I couldn't name the man who pushed Paul over. And if I'd talked, there would have been inquiries at Tor House, Reddelow would have been questioned and I think the situation would have become worse. There are times when its better to hold one's tongue. I decided that this was one.'

'Although Reddelow may have been responsible for the murder?' Gratton said harshly.

Grey looked at him intently.

'Gratton—you and your friends must understand the situation. Murder has been committed and might be again. Where are they? What happened—'

Grey broke off, backing swiftly to the window, holding the gun. Gratton darted a glance behind him; the handle of the door was turning. He thought of Fryer—and of Fryer's men. The tension was almost unbearable.

The door burst open.

'Don't move!' snapped Grey. 'Don't—'

'Dear old hermit,' breathed Claude, 'what a greeting! You wouldn't keep me in the draughty passage, would you?' Claude, dishevelled, with smears of dirt over his face and a rent in the shoulder of his coat, came in and closed the door gently behind him.

He took a step forward.

'Stay where you are!' snapped Grey.

A hand appeared at the window!

Gratton caught his breath, as the hand drew nearer to Grey's right arm. With one sharp, unexpected movement the gun was dislodged and fell to the floor. The unseen man pushed aside the curtains and climbed into the room.

'Nice work, Pat,' praised Claude.

Dawlish grinned across at Gratton.

Realising that he had no chance to escape, Grey talked freely—up to a point. He repeated everything he had said to Gratton, swore that he had no idea of what the mystery was about, and refused point-blank to explain his interest in Sir Henry Reddelow.

Gratton was a long time getting to sleep that night, his mind was a whirl of imperfectly answered questions. At the back of everything was an image of Judy Bell, her obvious weariness; her fear; and the loveliness of her eyes. He could not rid himself of a desperate anxiety for her.

Grey had been 'allowed' to go; and Jeremy, who had arrived soon after Dawlish, had followed him.

Beresford had not returned to the *Lobster Pot* but had telephoned to say that he was watching Tor House from a clump of trees half-way up the hill.

Dawlish, Jeremy, and Claude had achieved one thing in the caves; they had discovered that the cliffs were honeycombed with them, and that it was possible to walk underground to within a few hundred yards of Tor House. They reached the open air in the cliffside beneath the house, and Dawlish had said:

'Not a nice spot, Toby. There we were, directly above a whirlpool which I'm told is the biggest in these parts, and pretty deadly.'

He had not mentioned Paul, although by then Grey had told him of the murder.

Gratton tossed and turned, remembering that Dawlish had made little comment about Judy's visit and her appeal. This reticence could mean that Dawlish thought that the girl was not to be trusted. Yet could anyone doubt her anguish?

Did she know that Paul was dead?

Was that what had frightened her?

At last, he feel asleep.

Gratton awoke to a dull morning, made more so by a thin drizzle of rain. He felt a heavy sense of depression; this thing was too much for them, and yet—what would happen if they did inform the police? Could the police help Judy, now?

The door opened abruptly, and Claude poked his head in.

''Morning, Toby I All having breakfast together in half-an-hour's time. I'll bang on the door when I'm out of the bathroom.'

He waved a hand, and withdrew.

A tepid bath did not do much to bring Gratton to a more

cheerful frame of mind. He felt stiff from the unusual exertions of the night before, as he went downstairs.

Dawlish and Beresford were already at the table, looking fresh and rested.

Gratton thawed a little at the sight of a huge breakfast.

'Three men in a cave would like some of this,' he remarked, but the comment was not so sour as it would have been five minutes before.

Dawlish chuckled.

'They've had theirs,' he declared. 'Bread, cheese and water, and they ought to think themselves lucky to get the cheese. I went along myself, just before dawn,' he added. 'Tim's had his breakfast and is now watching Tor House. We're leaving the hermit for a bit, he didn't tell you anything else, I suppose?'

'No,' said Gratton. 'You know as much as I do.'

The bacon was crisp, the toast plentiful, and the coffee hot. He hadn't realised how hungry he was.

Dawlish waited until he had nearly finished, before pushing his chair back. 'Well, now, a plan of action is called for, and boldness seems the best course. I'm going to see Reddelow this morning. Coming?' Gratton put his coffee cup down with dangerous haste.

'Ted is going to keep watch,' Dawlish went on, 'his leg prevents him from being too active and we may have to run. The idea is simple: see Reddelow, and demand an audience with Judy. Just to see how it goes,' he added. 'I—hallo,' he broke off, at a tap on the door. 'Come in!'

The receptionist appeared.

'Mr. Dawlish, there is a telephone call from London for you,' he said, 'a Mr. Plomley. Will you take it?'

Dawlish frowned; obviously he had not expected to hear from Plomley.

'Yes,' he said. 'Thanks.'

'Odd,' remarked Beresford as the big man went out of the room. 'Plomley isn't supposed to know where to find us. Worrying. I hope Felicity's all right.'

'Why shouldn't she be?'

'Dawlish has a theory that the enemy always strikes at the weakest spot. That's why he didn't want Felicity to know where we were coming, and why he left Dick Plomley to look after her.'

Gratton caught some of Beresford's unease. Both of them listened intently for Dawlish's return. Then Beresford, facing the window, suddenly went rigid.

'What—' began Gratton.

He turned his head and saw, walking towards the front door, *Fryer*.

CHAPTER FIFTEEN

FAT FRYER IS CONFIDENT

Fryer passed the window without glancing into the room, and his passing seemed to cast a shadow over the table. Beresford rose to his feet and limped across to the door.

He put out a hand to take the handle, then drew back.

'Better see how it works out,' he muttered.

'Why not listen to what Fryer says in the hall?' asked Gratton.

He pushed past Beresford and opened the door. Between the morning-room and the hall was a short, narrow passage, gloomy at all times and especially so on this drab morning.

Fryer spoke.

'You have a Mr. Dawlish staying here.'

'That is so, sir.'

'I want to see him.'

'At the moment, he is on the telephone in his room,' said the receptionist, 'but he will be down in a few minutes, sir, he hasn't yet finished his breakfast. If you will please take a seat . . .'

'I'll go up,' said Fryer.

'I think perhaps if you wait—'

'I'm in a hurry,' growled Fryer, 'and—'

'I shouldn't hurry too much,' said Beresford, from Gratton's side. 'Dawlish will be down in a minute, come and have a cup of coffee while you're waiting.' He moved forward, blocking the doorway leading to the stairs. Strange that Fryer had dared to come here alone. Possibly he had a bodyguard outside.

Gratton slipped into the porch. The fine rain fell on to his face, like the spray from the waterfall. He looked at the car, a large Austin; a chauffeur sat at the wheel, reading a newspaper. No one else was in sight—but yes, someone was there; the 'hermit' stood in a doorway at the other side of the road, and in another stood Claude!

Gratton hurried back to the morning-room; there was no sign of Dawlish.

Fryer stood in the window, with a cup of coffee in his hand. Whatever else, one had to admire the fat man's nerve.

'Perhaps you will be kind enough to send Gratton upstairs to tell Dawlish I want to see him.'

Beresford grinned.

'No page boys here, Fryer! Gratton stays, and Dawlish will come in his own good time.'

'Beresford,' Fryer said harshly. 'You once lost a leg in what Dawlish called an "affair", didn't you? I took no part in that, but I heard about it. There might be other, equally unpleasant accidents. Don't do anything foolish.'

'My dear man! gasped Beresford. 'The very idea! *Foolish?*'

Fryer exclaimed in exasperation, and turned to Gratton.

'Gratton, you are not really one of these men,' he said. 'You don't know the risks you're running. They are, in fact, asking you to stick your head in a noose. Before they've finished they'll have blood on their hands, and that means that they and their accomplices will pay—' Fryer's voice sank theatrically—'the ultimate penalty.'

In spite of himself Gratton felt the stirring of disquiet.

'If you have any sense. you will back out,' Fryer went on. 'You would be much wiser to go to the police than to continue to act as a stooge for these lunatics.'

'Now that *really* is altruistic advice!' exclaimed Beresford in mock admiration. 'And you so nervous of the police!'

Fryer thrust his head forward.

'Gratton, if you tell the police what has happened, they will tell you that you have aligned yourself with a gang of hooligans who set the law at naught, and—'

Gratton exclaimed: 'Surely you're forgetting that my evidence—'

'Your evidence would not be of the slightest danger to me,' said Fryer confidently. 'I shall give evidence—and find others to support it—that I was not at the house near Harrow the night before last. A man cannot be in two places at the same time and I shall be able to *prove* that it was a case of mistaken identity.'

Fryer finished his coffee, and looked at his watch.

'I've no more time to waste! If Dawlish—'

'Looking for me?' asked Dawlish.

Gratton's heart missed a beat, for Dawlish had made not the slightest sound as he opened the door and came in. Now he closed the door gently behind him.

'Because I'm looking for you,' he declared.

The big man's face was set, there was a steely glint in his eyes.

'Dawlish, I've come to warn you. I don't want to be unpleasant, but—'

'Well, well,' said Dawlish. 'The sentiment does you credit. I wonder if Paul recognised it!'

'I cannot be held responsible for every man who falls over a cliff!'

'Falls?' asked Dawlish—'or was pushed? May I ask if you kidnapped my wife in the same spirit of pleasantness?'

Utter silence fell upon the four men in the room.

That Felicity Dawlish had fallen into Fryer's hands explained this new Dawlish, the hardness of his eyes and the grimness of his voice. And now Fryer was frightened.

Something glittered in Dawlish's fingers.

A knife!

He held it between thumb and forefinger, the blade pointing towards Fryer's stomach. Fryer's breathing became hoarse and laboured, he threw out a hand in quick repudiation.

'I can do a lot of damage with this knife, Fryer,' said Dawlish. 'You've spent some time in the East, haven't you? You know some of the nice little disembowelling tricks they get up to out there.'

'Dawlish! I—I—'

'Think about it,' Dawlish said, 'because that's what will happen to you if any harm comes to my wife.'

'That—that's up to you,' muttered Fryer. 'I won't hurt her, if you—'

'You won't hurt her, whatever I do,' said Dawlish, 'because police or no police, you won't escape me if you do her any harm.'

Fryer gave a little, choking cry; and backed against the window.

'Understand?' asked Dawlish, harshly.

'You—you daren't—'

'I'll dare anything if you drive me to it,' Dawlish said. 'Get it out of your head that you can deliver any ultimatum, Fryer. Why did you come here?'

Fryer licked his lips.

'I—Dawlish, there's no point in behaving like this! I—I'm not responsible for—'

'Are you trying to tell me that you're acting under orders?' asked Dawlish softly.

'Yes, I—'

'Whose orders?'

Fryer licked his lips. 'Dawlish, I can't help myself, I've got to do this. I have to do what I'm told. And you'll only make the situation worse if you stay down here. Be sensible, return to London and your wife will join you. You can't *do* anything.'

'No?' said Dawlish raising his eyebrows. 'Yet I've caught three of your key men. And even the most reliable men will sometimes talk.'

Fryer said desperately: 'Dawlish, you've got to release those men! If they're not free by this afternoon, I—I can't be responsible for what happens to your wife, I tell you it won't be in my hands!' Sweat was standing out on Fryer's lips and forehead. 'It won't be any use blaming me, Dawlish. Release the men, go back to London, take all the others with you, and then—'

'And then you'll be able to go ahead with your nice little plot that no one knows anything about,' said Dawlish. 'No, no, Fryer. I'm going to see it through. But remember this—if I lose, it'll be the end for you. The police will know quickly enough then. I've arranged it. Now go back and tell your Boss.'

Fryer muttered: 'Dawlish, you must listen to reason, I've warned you—'

'Get out,' said Dawlish. He shot out his hand, gripped the fat man by the shoulder, and pushed him towards the door.

'I tell you—' began Fryer.

'Out!' rumbled Beresford.

Dawlish stepped to the window. Beresford joined him on one side and Gratton on the other.

A car door slammed.

Beresford stirred. 'No so good,' he said.

'No. Any coffee left?' Dawlish asked absently. 'Plomley telephoned to tell me that Felicity had left her hotel at half-past five this morning and hadn't been seen since. I—' he broke off, while Gratton poured out the coffee. 'Thanks,' he said. 'Well, it's happened and we've got to face it. I don't think we need change any plans, a visit to Reddelow's the next step.'

'But surely you can't try to handle this yourself *now*,' protested Gratton hotly. 'It was bad enough before, but if your wife's in danger—'

'All the more reason why we should handle it,' said Dawlish. He looked wonderingly at his coffee cup. 'What the devil am I drinking this for—any beer, Ted?'

'Gallons. Upstairs.'

'Then let's go upstairs,' said Dawlish.

As they passed through the hall, Claude joined them.

'I don't know what you did to Fryer,' Claude said, 'but he seemed to be pretty deflated.'

'It's Fel,' said Beresford.

'Oh. So that's the way it is.'

Dawlish said: 'According to Fryer she's somewhere near London, but who can believe him?' He frowned. 'I wonder if the power behind this affair is Reddelow? George Grey did rather overdo that bit about him being more sinned against than sinning.'

Gratton nodded.

'That may be what all of them want us to believe,' said Dawlish. He lit a cigarette, then finished his beer. 'Time we were up and doing. Coming with me to Tor House, Toby?'

'Not fair,' murmured Claude. 'My turn.'

'You'll stay here, old chap, in case anything turns up,' said Dawlish. 'Ted, will you amble along ahead and tell Tim that we're going. And ask Tim to keep an eye on our hermit, while you keep watch on Tor House from the thicket. Seems the best way to split up,' he added reflectively. 'We've got to count Freddie out, I suppose?'

'A torn ligament. Won't walk for a week or more,' Claude said. 'Pretty browned off but bearing up. Er—are you wise to go to Tor House? Spider and fly business all over again, you know.'

Dawlish grinned.

'You may be right! But I'm going to see Reddelow and I'm going to see Judy, and I'll be surprised if one of them doesn't talk. I shall try to bring Judy away,' he added calmly.

Beresford said: 'Going to try any rough stuff?'

'That depends on what they try. I'll go prepared, anyhow. Come on, Toby.'

As they drew nearer to the house, Gratton was able to see more clearly the wild nature of the countryside. Tor House seemed to have been built on the bleakest spot near Merrance; they could see the village to the left, but in front of them the cliff dropped down on to jagged rocks and, quite clearly through the misty drizzle, Gratton could see the whirlpool at the foot of the cliff. The road grew steeper. Now all there was between them and the house was the coarse grass and a wide patch of heather. The house itself was surrounded by a stone wall. Tall wrought iron gates stood open. As Gratton went past them he wondered whether Dawlish was about to make a mistake which they would never be able to rectify—whether, in fact, those gates would close on them for ever.

The house, too, was built of stone, an ugly building with high, inaccessible windows.

As Gratton pulled up, the front door opened.

CHAPTER SIXTEEN

TOR HOUSE

A man stood by the open door, a short, sallow, grim-looking man with jet black hair. He was dressed in the conventional, man-servant's attire, and stood respectfully enough as Dawlish and Gratton approached him.

'Good-morning, gentlemen,' his voice was harsh. 'I am afraid that—'

'We have come to see Sir Henry,' Dawlish interrupted.

'So I inferred, sir. And I was about to inform you that Sir Henry is indisposed, and is unable to see anyone.'

'Tell Sir Henry that Mr. Patrick Dawlish and Mr. Tobias Gratton wish to see him,' said Dawlish authoritatively.

He swept the man aside and entered the house.

Four closed doors led from the hall; no one was in sight; yet Gratton felt that they were being watched. Someone was on the landing; he could see the face, a pale blur in the shadows. It was a large landing with a railed gallery, hung with dark and gloomy portraits.

'Tell Sir Henry,' said Dawlish curtly.

The man shrugged his shoulders sullenly and walked

away. He tapped at one of the doors, and Fryer's voice said 'Come in'.

Dawlish and Gratton could hear a muttered argument from the room into which the footman had gone; was Reddelow refusing to see them and Fryer trying to persuade him? If so, was Reddelow *frightened* of him? Had George Grey been right when he had suggested that the man was being blackmailed?

Seconds flew; minutes passed . . .

'*Dawlish!*'

Another whisper came from above their heads; they could see nothing—but yes, they could: Judy Bell was leaning over the gallery!

'*Mr. Dawlish.*'

Dawlish said: 'Wait here, Toby, be prepared for anything. Open the front door.' He moved as he spoke, striding towards the stairs and mounting them three at a time.

Judy's voice came clearly to Gratton as he opened the door. 'No, no, no!'

The next moment Dawlish had her in his arms and was running downstairs.

'Start the car!'

Gratton hurried out, and slid into the driving seat, pulling the self-starter. The engine hummed as Dawlish came out of the house. Judy was struggling and striking at Dawlish's face, but it appeared to have no effect whatever. He dumped her into the back of the car and climbed in after her. The engine kicked as Gratton swung the wheel.

'Let me go!' cried Judy, 'let me—'

The car was now heading for the gates at thirty miles an hour down the steep drive. A hundred yards to go, and—

A man shouted from the house!

'Stop! Dawlish! Stop!'

'Hurry!' Dawlish snapped to Gratton. 'If we can get out of the grounds—'

He stopped abruptly—and Gratton's heart leapt to his mouth. *The gates were beginning to close.* No one was near them; no one had touched them; but they were moving slowly, and he was still fifty yards away, he couldn't hope to get through. His foot went down on the brake, but he lifted it swiftly and swung the wheel. The car jolted over a row of shrubs, tore over the garden, uprooting plants and dislodging stones.

Gratton drove to the extreme limit of the grounds, where the wall confronting them was considerably lower. Gratton looked round desperately, hoping to see another gate, but there was nothing—only the wall and the bleak hillside beyond.

Dawlish said: 'I'm going to jump out with her and get over the wall.'

'*Let me go!*' cried Judy.

'My dear girl,' said Dawlish, 'try to be reasonable. If you attempt to get away now, we'll both fall and break our necks.'

A shot ran out.

The sharp report made Gratton glance towards the house. A man at a first-floor window was levelling a gun towards the car and—*clang*! A bullet hit the wing. The wall was only a few yards away from them, and Gratton slowed to a standstill.

Dawlish scrambled to the roof of the car and from there to the top of the wall. Between them they hoisted the girl up, Gratton following. As they dropped to the other side, two shots rang out in rapid succession.

Gratton glanced towards the road.

Three men, two of them carrying guns, were coming towards them, cutting off their escape. Dawlish, the girl in his arms, made for the cliff.

Gratton remembered suddenly, and with terror, the whirl-pool and the sheer drop which they had seen from the road.

'Dawlish—the whirlpool!' he shouted.

CHAPTER SEVENTEEN

THE CLIFF

Dawlish half turned, urging him on.

He couldn't have heard aright, thought Gratton; yet he was racing towards the edge of the cliff as if knowing exactly what he was about. Now, he was heading straight for the ridge above the whirlpool. Gratton followed, the threat from the three approaching men lending wings to his feet, although he could not see how they were to escape.

Crack!

A bullet winged over his head. He glanced over his shoulder again. Two more men had appeared further down the hill, and the first three were spreading out, so that a cordon stretched from Tor House to the top of the cliff; escape that way was now impossible.

He saw that the village was enshrouded in misty rain; even the thicket was vague and half-hidden. Soon the hillside would be blotted out from the view of anyone in the village, taking away their only hope.

Dawlish was now nearing the cliff top.

The approaching men held their fire, as if they realised the inevitability of making captures. They were getting closer to one another, making the chances of slipping through them even slimmer. Dawlish would have to give up.

The big man stood on the edge of the cliff, looking down, as if searching for something. Gratton drew nearer, and shouted:

'We can't go back!'

Dawlish glanced round.

'We don't want to go back,' he said casually, 'we're going down. There's the spot.' He pointed. 'Get going Toby.'

Crack!

Gratton could hear the hissing, swirling water and see the fierce whirlpool, bubbling and seething, it was like a huge wheel, for ever revolving, in the centre an angry cauldron of boiling water. So fierce was the current that no one who fell from the cliff could avoid being drawn into the terrible vortex. There was only one way down—a narrow, rocky path leading to a still narrower ledge. If they reached that ledge they might be able to round the cliff at a point where it jutted out beyond the whirlpool, and reach safety.

He might be able to, but could Dawlish, burdened as he was with the girl?

Crack!

The men hunting them down had been firing at Dawlish, Gratton himself had been in little danger. But now Dawlish was only a few yards away from him.

'Get down!' cried Dawlish.

Gratton stepped over the edge of the cliff. His foot rested precariously on a small rock which jutted out; but it held. He went down slowly. This was worse, far worse, than the descent to the caves. Loose stones rolled from under his feet, once he dislodged a small boulder, which clattered down the steep face of the rock until it dropped into the whirlpool.

He seemed alone; terribly alone. Yet he would be safer if that were true. Dawlish was only a few yards above him. If he were hit, both he and Judy would topple into the sea, carrying him with them.

Crack-crack-crack-crack!

Gratton held on to a boulder, and turned round.

Dawlish was now beneath the level of the cliff, and safe from immediate danger. He had lifted the girl until she was over his shoulder, and he came down much more quickly than Gratton, surefooted and confident. He said calmly:

'Better hurry, old chap. Once we're on that ledge we'll be all right.'

Scrambling, clinging, enduring, Gratton reached the ledge; at the same time a shot rang out and dirt spurted up from the cliffside close to his hand. Dawlish was only a few yards behind him. The men above had reached the top of the cliff and were firing wildly; they would surely score a hit, just one would be enough.

'Hurry round!' snapped Dawlish.

Gratton edged his way along the ledge. Now Dawlish carried the girl in his arms again, and Gratton thought he knew why; hanging over his shoulder, she would have been the first victim of a shot.

Gratton glanced round at him.

He was putting the girl down on the ledge.

'Up to you now,' said Dawlish. 'Do what Gratton's doing, it's not difficult. I—ach!'

Dawlish staggered, shot out a hand and clutched a rock, saved himself from falling and stood quite still. The girl looked at him fearfully, but he waved her on.

Judy edged towards Gratton, who realised with great relief that he was now out of range from the top of the cliff; and the girl soon would be. But Dawlish stood there, an easy target; and blood was dropping from his right hand.

Gratton made another two yards, until both Dawlish and the girl were lost to sight. He went on. The ledge grew wider, and he could walk fairly easily now. He did not go far, but waited until Judy came in sight.

Why didn't Dawlish come? Why didn't . . .

Here he was!

The big man clung to the side of the cliff with his left hand; his right arm hung limp by his side. He looked deathly pale. He paused to wave Gratton on, and Gratton turned his back on them both and walked along the widening ledge.

Now he was immediately above the little cove.

A fall would still be fatal, for close to the foot of the cliffs the rocks were jagged; further along still, where the ledge narrowed again the drop was sheer into the calm sea. Gratton looked up. Above him the cliff was so steep that he did not think anyone standing on the top would be able to see him—or any of them. The immediate danger was past. There might be another way down to this ledge, or the men might follow them; but they had won some breathing space.

He leaned against the face of the cliff, and Judy joined him. He said nothing; both of them waited for Dawlish.

He came at last, crisp curly hair slightly ruffled, but the same carefree, debonair expression.

The drizzle still fell softly, and now Gratton realised that the rocks down which they had climbed had been slippery. It was hard to believe that all three of them had managed to get down.

He said abruptly: 'Let me have a look at your arm.'

'It's nothing much.'

'Let me have a look,' insisted Gratton, and Dawlish shrugged his shoulders and pulled back his sleeve. A bullet had gone through the fleshy part of his forearm, which was already swelling. Blood covered his hand and wrist.

Gratton took out a clean handkerchief, folded it, and tied it round the wound with a double knot.

'You'd better have the gun,' Dawlish said, 'two hands are better than one.' He turned to Judy, whose gaze was focussed on the distant sea. She was pale and drawn, as if filled with dark, secret thoughts and fears. Of what was she thinking? Why was she so afraid? Why had she tried again to warn them to leave the district?

'How bad is it?' Dawlish asked quietly.

She glanced at him.

'I've told you,' she said, 'we haven't a chance. I—never had a chance, but you would have been all right if you hadn't done this. What good do you think it's done?' she asked, passionately. 'What good *can* it do?'

'That's up to you,' said Dawlish. 'You know what they're doing, don't you?'

She said: 'Yes, I know, but I'm not going to tell you. It wouldn't help. We'll never get away from here,' she went on, 'they'll come out of the caves and prevent us from getting away whichever way we turn.'

'You're wrong, Judy,' Dawlish said. 'Two of my friends were watching from the thicket. They must have seen what happened. They'll hare down to the village and get a boat, and they'll come round this way. We hadn't a chance above the whirlpool, but it's all right here.'

'They won't have time,' Judy said doggedly.

Dawlish shrugged his shoulders.

'You'll see,' he said.

Gratton did not speak, but one question pressed insistently on his mind. Was Dawlish relying on Beresford and Jeremy getting a boat? Could he be sure they would do that? But—even if he were right, it would take them the better part of an hour; and that would be too long.

Judy said quietly:

'Don't you ever know when you're beaten?'

Dawlish said lightly: 'When, and if, that happens it's possible that I will. The trouble with you is that Fryer has persuaded you that we can't win. A matter of brainwashing.' He paused for a moment and then asked gently: 'Do you know that Fryer's men murdered Paul?'

Judy started violently.

Gratton watched her. So she hadn't realised that. Standing there with her lips parted and her eyes rounded in horror, she looked superbly beautiful. He would remember her with her dark hair tumbling to her shoulders and her cheeks whipped by the wind to his dying day.

He forgot where they were; and forgot their plight. Dawlish's friends might come; or Fryer's men might arrive first. They might never leave this spot alive, this might be their last day on earth—yet he could only stand and watch her, seeing the pulse fluttering in her forehead, guessing at the tempestuous thoughts which flashed through her mind.

'No,' she said at last in a strange, thin voice: 'No, that isn't true.'

'It's quite true,' insisted Dawlish.

'Then—' she began.

What she would have said, whether that information would have proved the turning point, Gratton never knew; but before she went on, two things happened. A small stone fell between Dawlish and Judy Bell; and something rumbled above their heads, like distant thunder.

All three looked up.

A little cascade of dirt and stones was falling and as they stared something large and dark loomed out of the mist and crashed towards them!

Dawlish uttered a sharp exclamation, flung his left arm round Judy and pushed her towards the face of the cliff. Gratton flattened himself against the rock; as he did so a huge boulder crashed on to the ledge, chippings and stones flew viciously, striking the side of the rock like shrapnel; the boulder rolled towards them and then, of its own volition, rolled away, reached the ledge and toppled over.

The stones stopped falling, the dust and dirt settled; all was silent except the splashing of the water on the beach below.

Dawlish said heavily: 'So that's the game.'

'I—knew they'd do—something like this,' Judy said.

The truth had been clear enough from the moment Gratton had started to think. The men above them knew where they were standing, and the boulder had been loosened until it fell; and others would follow. Even as Judy finished, the face of the rock seemed to quiver, and the preliminary cascade of stones and dirt hurtled down. With narrowed eyes, Gratton watched another huge boulder fall. Involuntarily he closed his eyes; when he opened them again the boulder was toppling over the edge, and the air was filled with dust and dirt.

'There can't be many loose rocks up there,' said Dawlish absently.

'There are dozens,' said Judy emotionlessly.

'You insist on being cheerful, don't you?' said Dawlish briskly. 'Ted and Tim shouldn't be long,' he added, and looked towards the cliffs where they jutted out into the sea, hiding Merrance and the cove from sight. The boat—if one came—would have to sail round that promontory, and for all he knew, the currents might prevent a boat from coming this far.

The rumbling began afresh.

Gratton held his breath.

This time the crash, when the boulder fell, made the ledge shake under their feet. It was a huge rock, and must weigh several tons. As it toppled into the sea the splash sent a spray of water on to their faces.

'Look!' gasped Judy.

She pointed a quivering finger towards the edge of the ledge; it was cracked and as they looked the crack widened, and a large piece broke from it and fell. After the noise and the splashing had quietened, they saw that a third of the ledge had completely disappeared.

The silence was short-lived. The now familiar rumbling sounded again above their heads.

Instinctively, they turned their faces to the wall, but Gratton knew there was no hope. Judy had been right. The ledge would crack and crumble under the constant barrage.

Dawlish said lightly: 'I hope you two can swim.'

CHAPTER EIGHTEEN

THE SEA

No one spoke after the cryptic sentence, but the words echoed in Gratton's mind. 'I hope you two can swim.' That was the obvious, the only thing to try now, but—what hope was there? They had no knowledge of the currents; he wasn't a powerful swimmer, and Dawlish would not be able to make much headway with one arm useless. And Judy—

She began to kick off her shoes.

Gratton took off his shoes and coat, Dawlish, managing very well in spite of his wounded arm, stripped to singlet and trousers. There was a welcome lull in the bombardment as they prepared, but when Dawlish went forward cautiously, to spy out the best place to dive, the rumbling began again.

'We'll go between the showers,' Dawlish said.

He stood with his back against the face of the cliff, then ran forward; next moment, he plunged over. Gratton waited with clenched teeth; the splash came at last.

Judy picked her way across the ledge towards the spot which Dawlish had chosen. She stood poised; then with a single, graceful movement, put her hands above her head and dived.

As she did so, the rumbling started again.

Gratton, flat against the cliff, could not turn his face away. If the boulder fell near her, the splash, the suction, would create a vortex which would surely suck her down. He was rigid with fear; he ignored the first trickle of stones; he saw the boulder loom out of the mist; and a moment later it crashed twenty yards from where Judy had started.

Surely—surely that was far enough away from her.

Quickly, far from expertly, Gratton dived.

The sea was fifty feet below him. If a rock fell while he was close to the cliff he would have little chance. He cut through the water, desperation giving him extra strength. Not until he was thirty yards or more from the cliff did he pause, looking round for the others.

Thank God, Judy was some way ahead of him, making good speed; and Dawlish was a little way from her.

Gratton tried to calculate how far they would have to swim in order to reach Merrance Cove. By land it must be half a mile; by sea, probably twice as far. The promontory, which had looked fairly near from the cliff, now seemed an infinite distance away. He doubted whether he could keep going long enough to reach it; and he would have at least as far again to swim on the other side. He would never manage it.

Nonsense! He had to manage it, even if it took him all day, he had to keep afloat. That was the main thing—to keep afloat.

The last time he had looked, Dawlish and Judy had been immediately in front of him, but now they were some distance to his right. He couldn't understand it. They were swimming side by side; as if Judy had slowed down in order to keep pace with Dawlish. As he watched, he saw that although they were aiming at the same point as he, they were moving towards the right.

They were caught in a current!

The truth came upon him with a flash of dreadful understanding. Struggle as they might, they could not make headway. Dawlish was losing the the fight—he was ten feet or more away from Judy now, and being drawn remorselessly towards the whirlpool. Had he been able to use both arms he would have been safe, thought Gratton, and—Judy *was* safe. Yes, she was beyond the current. She had stopped; she was treading water and looking at Dawlish, her hair clinging close to her head and cheeks. She was calling—shouting! Gratton could just hear the echo of her voice across the water. She was encouraging Dawlish—no, she was shouting to *him*, pointing—pointing towards the left.

She meant that he should turn left and strike out along the side of the cliff, otherwise he would reach the current and be drawn away from all hope of safety.

Gratton raised a hand, to show Judy that he understood, and turned towards the cliff, swimming slowly, feeling a terrible dread. Dawlish hadn't a chance. Judy and he might get ashore, but not Dawlish.

Suddenly, he became aware of another sound; a staccato beat, as of an engine.

A motor launch was coming round the cliffs!

'All aboard the lugger,' cried Claude. 'Don't be awkward, Toby, the others were easy. Got him, Tim? One, two, three—heave! That's the spirit!'

Gratton collapsed in the bottom of the boat, shivering violently. He caught a glimpse of Dawlish sitting doubled up in the bows, and Judy near him, blue with cold. Something was pressed against his lips—hard and cold.

'Leave a spot for the others,' protested Claude. 'Take it easy, old boy. That's fine.'

Claude dropped a blanket over him, then turned to Judy and offered her another spot. Jeremy was at the engine.

'How's the whirlpool, Tim?'

'We're all right,' said Jeremy, still looking at the cliff, 'unless those beggars find our range.'

'Soon be out of their sight,' said Claude. 'Have a drop more, Pat, we won't mind if you get drunk. And then start counting your blessings, you all ought to be dead.'

Dawlish looked up. His eyes were bloodshot and his face haggard. Gratton realised what a terrific struggle he must have put up against the current.

He looked at Judy.

Wrapped in a blanket, she was squeezing the water from her hair. Beads of water trickled down her cheeks and nose, but she still looked lovely. He remembered the way she had dived, judging the distance calmly, dispassionately.

She glanced at him and smiled.

'Feeling all right?' he asked in a croaking voice.

'Yes, thanks.'

Ridiculous things, words, at times like this.

Jeremy said suddenly:

'We'll be ashore in ten minutes. There's a small jetty belonging to the *Lobster Pot*, and a road runs to the back of the pub. There shouldn't be anybody there.'

'Good work,' said Dawlish.

Judy said: 'Are you really going to keep this from the authorities Mr. Dawlish?'

'Why, yes,' said Dawlish. 'But if you try to get away again, if you give us the slip once more Judy, that's *finis*. I'll hand the whole thing over to the police, so help me!'

Gratton rubbed himself down vigorously after a hot bath,

glowing all over. He wrapped a borrowed dressing-gown round him, and went across to the double room, which was the meeting-place for them all. Dawlish was there, sitting in a large chair which had been brought up from the lounge. Beresford sat in a window seat, Claude swung his legs from a table and held up a bottle of local brew.

'Ready for it now, Toby?'

'Yes, thanks,' said Gratton. 'Where's Judy?'

Claude beamed. 'Don't worry about Judy. I think she'll play from now on.'

'I wonder,' said Gratton.

'We can only try to make her see sense,' Dawlish said slowly. 'There must be something pretty grim to make the girl behave as she does, unless—' He paused. 'Unless she's really working with Fryer.'

He turned to Claude. 'You say that Grey repeated his assertion that Reddelow's being blackmailed?'

'Yes, and convincingly enough. Had quite a chat with him. Rather liked the fellow.'

Gratton listened with only half his attention. Now and again an emotion not far removed from anger surged through him; how could they behave so facetiously after what had happened? Yet it *was* understandable; and when it came to action, all of them were astonishing in their speed and their quick-wittedness. Had that boat arrived ten minutes later, it would have been too late to save Dawlish.

When he thought of the incident at Tor House, Gratton marvelled at the speed of the decision and the execution of an idea which could only have flashed into Dawlish's mind when the girl had whispered from the gallery. From that moment he had seen Dawlish as a kind of superman. Nevertheless, he felt that things had gone far enough; indeed, too far. Dawlish was wrong in his blind obstinacy to withhold information from the police. Too many lives were at stake. Had Fryer's men had their way, three people would have been murdered that morning! Gratton steeled himself to speak calmly and rationally.

'Dawlish,' he began, 'don't you think this has gone far enough? I've played ball as long as I could, but now—the pace is altogether too fierce. At first Fryer was content to try and frighten us, but now he's out for cold-blooded murder. *Murder*, Dawlish; and he has at least twice as many men as we have!'

He broke off, at a tap on the door, followed by the entry of the hermit, smiling faintly. Gratton felt at once that he came with news; and that the news was bad. Grey, taking his time, looked from one to the other, his gaze eventually resting on Dawlish.

'I come in peace,' he said at last.

'All right, the parley's on,' Dawlish answered impatiently. 'What's the message?'

'You won't like it,' said Grey. 'I don't know that I do. The telephone cable between here and the rest of the country has been damaged. A storm's blowing up, and we're going to to be cut off by the sea within the next hour—if we're not already. There's only one road for cars out of Merrance. Two or three of Fryer's men are up there at this moment. It wouldn't surprise me if they're planning to block it.'

He paused; but no one spoke.

A gust of wind howled round the house and the windows rattled. Downstairs, the gong rang for luncheon. The four men watched George Grey in silence.

'Well, what are you going to do?' he asked.

A dull roar, coming from some way off, made him rush towards the window, and thrust it open, Dawlish and the others in his wake.

All of them could see the hill road, just visible through the driving rain. It was covered with a pall of smoke, and Gratton knew that it had been blown up.

CHAPTER NINETEEN

HEMMED IN

The smoke rose sluggishly into the air and then began to settle.

George Grey was the first to move away from the window.

'Well, that's that,' he said. 'The man certainly means business. I was about to tell you that Fryer has schemed to get the two younger policemen out of the village, the only one left being pretty nearly senile. So, whatever your decision about seeking police aid Dawlish, it's now too late to get it.'

Dawlish gave a half-smile.

'It looks like it,' he said. 'How much more do you know?'

'Nothing,' said Grey.

'Indeed. I find that hard to believe.' Dawlish looked at him narrowly. 'For instance, how did you learn what you've just reported?'

'A mere matter of intelligent observation,' Grey said a little smugly. 'It's fairly easy to see that half a dozen armed men could hem Merrance in. They could be placed at vantage points on the hills, and pick off anyone who tried to get through. It would be possible to slip out after dark, of course, but whatever Fryer is up to, won't take long. I know very little, but I can guess more.'

'Guess on,' said Dawlish.

Grey shrugged his shoulders.

'I think Fryer will send you an ultimatum. I think he'll tell you to go to Tor House and take all the others with you, and he'll threaten something pretty grisly unless you do.'

'Such as?'

'As to that, your guess is as good as mine, but let us say, a threat to plant another charge of T.N.T. in the middle of the town.'

Gratton exclaimed: 'Surely not—'

Grey swung round on him.

'Haven't you guessed yet that Fryer is a desperate man? You've driven him into a corner, and he's determined to get what he wants. I don't know who's with him in this, but it's obvious that a lot is at stake, and he'll take desperate steps to cover himself. Don't you agree, Dawlish?' he demanded abruptly.

'It wouldn't surprise me,' Dawlish agreed. 'I take it you're on our side?'

'I am.'

'Then a little explanation won't come amiss,' said Dawlish. 'You're a—'

'What the devil does it matter what Grey tells us about himself,' snapped Gratton hotly. 'That's only wasting time. We've got to do something.'

'Ah, yes,' said Dawlish. 'Something. The question is, what? We're stuck. We're hemmed in. Merrance is cut off from the rest of the country and will remain so for several hours. What we do will have to be based on what Fryer does—we've got to wait until his next move.'

'It's fantastic!'

'Certainly it is,' said Dawlish, 'but it's no use getting worked up about it. Fryer's burned his boats. He wants only a few hours to complete the unholy business, and he's gained those few hours. Grey, what's your interest in this affair?'

He was right, Gratton admitted grudgingly.

They had to wait for Fryer.

Grey took his old, burnt pipe from his pocket and began to fill it, just as he had done when he had enabled Judy to escape the night before. Once again he held the stage, and he behaved as if he knew it, and was determined to stay there for as long as he could. The business of lighting the pipe completed, he said quietly:

'Reddelow is my father.'

Few words could have had a more startling effect; every eye was turned towards the man who had called himself 'George Grey'.

He went on: 'My father is a conventional Civil Servant, one of the hierarchy at Whitehall, and I've always been a bit of a rolling stone. We quarrelled years ago. One thing led to another, and I flung out of Tor House on my twenty-first birthday. I haven't been back there since. But—I'm fond of the old man.'

Dawlish nodded.

'My father is—or was—a wealthy man, but money has never interested me very much,' said Grey. 'I've knocked around the world and done well enough for myself, and I've had an insight into a lot of funny business one way and another, but—the pull of Merrance got me a few months ago, and I decided to come down here and see how things were. An old servant at Tor House who remembered me didn't lose any time in telling me that my father was a changed man, that his retirement had been forced on him, and that she thought he was being black-mailed. She mentioned the name Fryer. Now I'd heard of Fryer,' he added, 'and what I'd heard wasn't good.'

'White slaving, drugs, smuggling, take your pick,' murmured Dawlish.

'Exactly. I began to put two and two together. You've realised, of course, that this place would be ideal for smuggling. Big stores could be held in the caves and Tor House used as head-quarters. I thought that was the game. But now I'm not so sure, or where the girl comes in.'

'A crucial point,' said Dawlish, 'in a very queer business.'

Grey said abruptly:

'What convinced you that it was a bad thing to go to the police?'

Dawlish said: 'It wasn't a "what", but a "who". Two "who's" in fact. Judy Bell and Paul. Paul was a British Consular official in Madrid. He was frantic about the need for secrecy. Just how he and Judy Bell got together I don't know, but—'

'I can tell you that,' said Judy.

She came in and closed the door.

Judy had borrowed a long, silk housecoat, that was too big for her, but very becoming. Her hair, still damp, curled on her fore-head in little half-moons. They looked up at her, all interested in their separate ways.

'Well Judy,' said Dawlish. 'What is the connection?'

'We met last year, at Monte Carlo,' Judy said quietly, 'and he rather lost his head. In more ways than one, because he lost heavily at the tables and he'd borrowed some of the consulate funds—'

'Phew!' whistled Claude. 'Taxpayer's pocket suffering again.'

'I gave him enough money to clear himself,' said Judy without paying any attention to the interruption, 'and he was embar-rassingly grateful. He told me that he had discovered a way of beating the rate of exchange. I wasn't interested—'

'Just a moment,' said Dawlish. 'You got Paul out of his jam, you say—how much was he in debt?'

'Several thousand pounds,' Judy replied calmly.

'And you were allowed to take only seventy-five pounds out of the country,' murmured Dawlish.

Judy laughed.

'It was quite above board I assure you. I have many investments in France and on the continent.'

'Proceed, golden girl,' murmured Claude.

It had been Paul who introduced her to Fryer.

She had disliked and mistrusted him from the beginning. He put several money-making propositions to her, but she refused to have anything to do with them.

She then met Sir Henry Reddelow who outlined a very different kind of scheme, its aim being to help displaced children on the continent. The plans, he told her, were already well advanced. Several large estates in France had been taken over, and they were to be turned into holiday and rest centres. He convinced her that the Governments of several European countries as well as Great Britain were interested and actually showed her letters from Government Departments.

Judy went on:

'The scheme was for all displaced persons, but mainly children, and I became deeply interested. I put up a large sum of money, and became President of the organisation. All went well until I found out that funds were being solicited from all over the world. And that the appeal was being made in my name! Of course, the whole business was a fraud. The bulk of the money was going to a few people, Fryer among them. There *were* these camps, but not one tenth of what there should have been in view of the amount of money collected. I threatened to tell the truth, and—Fryer turned up again.'

She broke off.

A waiter tapped at the door and called: 'Luncheon is served, please.' Dawlish called back, but no one moved.

'Then I learned more of the organisation,' Judy said huskily. 'It was a gigantic scheme to defeat the currency regulations; Fryer being the leading figure. The organisation was the window dressing; and it had been so cleverly arranged that I was hopelessly involved. There were threats on my life, if I dared to betray them. I told Freddie. On his advice I came to see you, but by then Fryer had scared me, and I hardly knew what I was doing. Paul was working for Fryer, he was being blackmailed because he had helped in the early days of the scheme, and had the truth about him been disclosed, he would have been dismissed the service. He asked me to meet him, saying he had some special information for me. That was the *rendezvous* I was to keep when you were to be in the flat, Mr. Dawlish.'

Dawlish nodded.

'But I didn't get to the flat,' said Judy simply. 'I hailed a taxi, and the driver took me to a house somewhere in Barnes. Fryer was there. So was Paul. Paul was allowed his freedom, I was kept locked up in a room most of the time, but—Paul helped me to escape. That was why I rang up asking you to meet me at the *Sola Club.*'

'Ah,' exclaimed Gratton.

'Why the *Sola?*' asked Dawlish.

'Because Paul said that someone there worked with Fryer. He didn't know who it was. After I arrived, I wandered through the Club until I came to a dressing-room. Someone hit me and—'

'*Damn his eyes!*' roared Dawlish, and to Gratton's astonishment he jumped to his feet. 'Where's my coat?' he cried. 'Tim—Toby—come on!'

Gratton said: 'What—'

'This breaks Freddie Appleyard's story wide open,' stormed Dawlish, 'we may get him at the nursing home.'

The sister on duty at the nursing home was astonished. Mr. Appleyard, whose ankle had been so badly hurt, had left quite early that morning. Sir Henry Reddelow's car had been sent for him, and the sister herself had recognised Reddelow's chauffeur. Mr. Appleyard, she said, seemed to have expected it. He had not even stayed for breakfast.

Dawlish returned to the *Lobster Pot* in a very thoughtful mood. The light-hearted way they had all delayed luncheon had not been approved by the hotel staff. Anxious to make amends Dawlish led the way to the room which had been set apart for them.

Hungry and relaxed, none of the others seemed surprised by the news of Freddie's disappearance. It had the advantage of making Judy's story more plausible.

And Fryer had made no move.

Dawlish was more affected by the development over Freddie than any of the others, and he toyed with roast mutton and green peas, taking little part in a general conversation which lacked the spontaneity which usually characterised him and his party.

At last, Dawlish said wearily:

'Well, Judy, you hadn't quite finished, had you?'

'I've told you how it started,' she said.

'And from there, I take it, Paul tried to help you, Fryer discovered it, and Paul was murdered. There may be a secondary reason, but Fryer couldn't rely on Paul to keep his mouth shut. Nor on you,' he went on, 'because he wasn't fooling in that attack on the cliff. You were the target. Killing Toby or me was a passing matter, we were merely making nuisances of ourselves. And although I put the breeze up him this morning, I don't doubt that Fryer thinks that he has me taped because of my wife.'

Judy stared. 'Where does she come in?'

Dawlish gave a harsh laugh.

'Didn't he tell you? I don't know where she is, only that she is in his hands, but—I'll have to work that out myself. It isn't the main problem. The main one is: why, after you'd arranged to meet us at the *Sola*, did you duck out and run away yourself? It doesn't make sense, Judy. And from that moment you became even more terrified of going to the police. Was it something which you discovered while you were at the *Sola*? Something so horrifying that you came here and—tried to persuade us to give everything up—so bad that you tried to scare us away from Tor House this morning? That "something", Judy, must be pretty bad. But you've got to talk about it now, you know. We can't let you keep it to yourself any longer. We're all in the same boat. If we ever get out of Merrance alive, we'll be lucky. We're going to try, even though it means breaking our necks in the trying, but we want to know exactly what we're fighting, we've been in the dark far too long.'

CHAPTER TWENTY

FRYER STRIKES

As Dawlish finished speaking, a blast of wind roared about the *Lobster Pot* and rain smashed against the rattling window. Yet no one looked round. Dawlish meant to hear Judy's story; Gratton wondered what he would do if she still refused to speak, if the motive for her silence was so strong that even now she had to hug her secret to herself.

Dawlish was a ruthless man . . . He spoke again.

'Judy, we must know.'

'Yes,' she said quietly. 'But it would have been far better if you'd never known, if I'd never come to you for help. My safety didn't matter—and doesn't matter.' For some reason she turned her glance on Gratton.

That was the moment when he knew that he was in love with her.

The gulf between them had never seemed wider. She had talked quietly enough about her wealth; yet their worlds were poles apart. That glance was almost the first spontaneous look of friendliness she had given him, and they seemed always to have been at cross-purposes. Yet he knew that he loved her.

'*Really, sir!*' The high-pitched voice of the receptionist filtered through the room, as footsteps sounded on the stairs. 'Really, sir, I must insist, Mr. Dawlish and his friends are not able to see you *now*. I will send up your name, but . . .'

Gratton jumped across to the door, and pulled it open. Fryer had swept his way to the very threshold.

Dawlish called out quietly:

'*All right, let him in.*'

'Well, well, if it isn't our old friend Fryer,' said Claude pleasantly, struggling to his feet. 'Come right in.'

Dawlish smiled up sardonically.

'You're late, Fryer,' he said, 'we've been waiting for you for a long time.'

Gratton said: 'Karloff's downstairs, Pat.'

'Oh, is he,' remarked Dawlish, raising one eyebrow. 'Pity. So you've found your little men and you're back at full strength, Fryer. All the more to frighten us with, but we take a lot of frightening. Have you released my wife yet?'

Fryer said: 'Your wife will no longer matter to you, Dawlish.'

Gratton stood quite still, watching the antagonists. A quick glance round the room had shown him that Judy had gone. He was puzzled, and yet relieved by her disappearance; and he thought that Fryer was more than disconcerted by it.

'You won't leave Merrance alive,' Fryer declared. He shrugged his shoulders. 'And that goes for all of you,' he added harshly.

'We are terrified,' murmured Dawlish. 'Can't you see us trembling?'

Fryer said:

'You think you're funny and you think you're brave, but you're neither. When you took the girl away from Tor House, you signed your own death warrants.'

'Dear me,' said Dawlish. 'So Judy's as important as all that. Good thing we put her in a place of safety,' he added.

'No one in Merrance is safe,' said Fryer. 'You had your chance, Dawlish, and you threw it away. Where is the girl?'

'Round and about,' Dawlish said airily.

'I want to know—'

'I'm sure you do,' said Dawlish kindly. 'But aren't you a little muddled? You say we're not going to leave Merrance alive—'

'And you won't!'

'Possibly not,' agreed Dawlish calmly, 'but as we're doomed anyhow, why should we do anything to help you find Judy?'

Fryer snapped: 'This hotel is surrounded by my men!'

'That won't do the hotel much harm,' said Dawlish. 'It's seen bad little men before from time to time, and the men it is who've died!'

Fryer's lips quivered with suppressed temper; while Gratton tried to understand why Dawlish was baiting him. What good could come out of it, short of putting Fryer in a towering rage, and Fryer in a towering rage would probably be even more dangerous than Fryer satisfied.

'Where—is—the—girl?' demanded Fryer.

'So sorry to disappoint you, but she isn't available. As you see, she has gone.'

'She couldn't have left Merrance,' said Fryer. But it seemed that some of his confidence had oozed away.

'So she couldn't have left Merrance,' echoed Dawlish. He grinned. 'We must admit you're an excellent authority, but not'—he shook his head—'infallible.'

Fryer said sharply: 'We've talked enough. Where's the girl?'

'Where's my wife?' countered Dawlish.

'Dawlish,' said Fryer softly, 'I want Judith Bell; and I want you and your friends. *All* of you are coming to Tor House with me. If you don't—'

'Ah,' said Dawlish, 'now we're coming to the motto in the cracker!'

'If you don't,' repeated Fryer, 'I shall give Rudden an order which will kill a hundred people in this village.'

Gratton felt himself go cold.

Beresford stood up abruptly, and Tim Jeremy opened the door and looked into the passage. So Karloff's name was Rudden, and he was guarding the door in person. It occurred to Gratton that they were now altogether and completely at this man's mercy. And he was sure that Fryer meant what he said.

Dawlish said: 'And how is this to be done, Fryer?'

'It is now five minutes to three,' said Fryer, glancing at his watch. 'At two-forty-five, over a hundred women from the village gathered in the Town Hall for a monthly meeting. Beneath the floor of the meeting room there is a charge of T.N.T. which will blow the building sky-high. That's how serious I am, Dawlish. Now—*where's the girl?*'

'I don't know.'

'Don't lie to me!'

'I tell you I don't know,' said Dawlish. 'We brought her ashore, and left her to have a bath. She vanished.' He leaned forward, earnest now, and sober of voice. 'She's pretty slippery when she sets her mind to it, this isn't the first time she's run out on us.'

'I don't believe you,' said Fryer.

Gratton thought: 'It won't work, Dawlish won't get away with this.' His thoughts roamed; tormented thoughts now; of the hundred women gathered in one room, of the horror that would come if Fryer carried out his threat. *Dare* he do that? Even if Dawlish withstood the pressure, would Fryer take such a step?

'I can't *make* you believe me,' said Dawlish evenly, 'or alter facts to suit your temper.'

'I see,' said Fryer, and suddenly raised his voice. 'Rudden! Show Dawlish that we mean what we say.'

'O.K.' Rudden's footsteps could be heard running down the stairs. There was a tense silence broken at last by Dawlish.

'I should be very careful, Fryer,' he said harshly.

'I've given you enough warning,' Fryer growled.

Claude looked him over speculatively.

'We could dot him one, Pat,' he suggested.

'Not a bad idea,' said Jeremy, smiling.

Fryer said waspishly: 'It should be needless to say that if I do not leave here safely there will be unpleasant repercussions.'

Dawlish said: 'You know, Fryer, you've miscalculated: badly. You can wipe us out, kill a hundred harmless women, crush the spirit and the life out of Judy Bell. You can do all that—and yet the law will catch up with you. Because, whatever happens down here now, you're finished. The police aren't fools. And when they discover that the telegraph cable was cut and the top road blown up, they won't rest until they have found out why, and who did it. Then, there are bodies. One man can fall over the cliff and when his body's washed up, it can be called an accident, but half-a-dozen—that's a very different matter. Think again, Fryer. Think again.'

A sudden roar blasted the quiet of the room, drowning his voice. The windows and the floor shook. Beresford was flung forward from the window, which bulged in, then broke with a terrific crack. Glass flew in all directions, doors banged; and women began to scream.

Fryer said:

'That was an empty shop, Dawlish. The next one will be occupied. And I'm very much afraid that it is you who have miscalculated. Your bodies won't be found. They'll be sealed up inside the caves. We're leaving Merrance. We'll be away before dawn tomorrow.' When Dawlish did not answer, he went on, his voice raised to a louder note because of the shouting outside, and the sound of people racing past the inn towards the scene of the explosion. Smoke billowed into the room and the smell of burning was almost suffocating.

Fryer said sneeringly: 'Do you intend to let a hundred women die just to save your own skin, Dawlish? In five minutes, I shall give Rudden another signal, and that will be the last one. One—hundred—women! Dawlish—where is Judy Bell?'

Where *was* Judy?

If she could hear what was being said, if she knew that the explosion was the result of Fryer's orders, how could she keep out of sight? If she was not here, then how had Dawlish managed to get her out of the room? Even if she had left by the window, wouldn't Fryer's men have seen her and reported by now?

Why was this happening? What made Fryer take such terrible decisions, and why was he so determined that Dawlish and the others should go with him? If he planned their murder, why not kill them here and now? If he could blow up a shop he could blow up the *Lobster Pot*. Where was the logic in this crazy violence?

Gratton tried to clear his mind of confusion—and as he stood there, impotent, inwardly fuming and desperately afraid for others, no longer for himself, he felt Claude touch his hand—perhaps with a little gesture of reassurance.

But it was more than that. Claude was slipping a small, lightly-rolled cylinder of paper into his palm.

Automatically, Gratton's fingers closed over it. What did it contain? Was it—*poison*? Had Dawlish always known there might be complete disaster, and had he prepared the easy way out for them?

Dawlish stood up slowly.

'All right, Fryer,' he said, 'we'll come, but we can't bring Judy, we don't know where she is.'

Now that he had won the battle, Fryer seemed supremely confident. He did not appear to be greatly worried about Judy's disappearance, although he showed a cold determination to find her. As Gratton, Dawlish, Beresford and Jeremy were led downstairs, he told Rudden to search every room in the hotel.

'Telephone me as soon as you've found her,' he ordered.

Three cars stood outside the *Lobster Pot*. Gratton and Dawlish were ordered to get into one, and they obeyed without argument. Until that moment, Gratton expected Dawlish to make a dash for it, but Dawlish now seemed resigned to the inevitable. He looked blankly in front of him, paying no attention at all to Gratton.

A man took the wheel; another sat beside him, and the car moved off.

Gratton stared at the throng about the burning wreckage. None of them took any notice of this car or the others which followed it. Six men were being forced away from the village at the point of a gun, and no one paid the slightest attention, or had the faintest suspicion of what was happening.

To Gratton, there seemed no hope at all. He was tormented by the thought of Judy. Where was she? How had Dawlish managed to get her out of the room? Was there any chance of her eluding Fryer?

Rain smashed against the windscreen and the windows on Gratton's side of the car. He could only see a few yards ahead.

Suddenly, Dawlish's hand closed over his knee; a quick, tight grip, and then the hand was taken away. Gratton glanced at him, but the big man's expression had not changed, and yet the pressure of his hand had seemed to say: 'We're not finished yet.'

The car lurched over the rough road, the wind howled and the rain hissed and splashed about them. Gratton saw the iron gates, which had closed on him only a few hours before. As soon as they were through the gateway, his last flicker of hope seemed to die.

But the cylinder remained in his pocket.

CHAPTER TWENTY-ONE

MESSAGE

The great hall was dark and gloomy, the staircase and landing filled with shadows. Gratton stared up at the gallery, where he had seen Judy. It seemed an age ago; yet it was barely six hours since he had been here! He stood by Dawlish's side, until one of the men from the car came in, carrying a gun.

'Upstairs,' he said.

Both of them obeyed.

They were forced along a narrow passage and up a second flight of stairs at the end of it.

The man who had spoken led the way into a succession of rooms exhibiting in glass cases all that was macabre and horrifying. Shuddering, Gratton turned his eyes from the bones and skulls and gruesome skeletons cleft with spears. Apparently each member of the party was to be left in solitude. Gratton was thankful to find his room held only flints and bronze coins, bowls and pitchers, all neatly labelled.

The door securely locked, Gratton was left alone.

One—hundred—women—butchered!

He mustn't think about it, nor of Judy, his love.

With none too steady hand he took out his cigarettes, lit one and put his case and lighter away. He would like to know what Fryer was planning, and why all this had come about. Even if it were the last thing revealed to him, he would like to know that.

No point, now, in thinking that if they had gone to the police in the beginning, this might never have happened. Why had Dawlish and Judy been so sure that it was the wrong thing to do?

Did Dawlish *know* anything?

He—

Fool! He dug his hand into his pocket, suddenly trembling, remembering the cylinder. His fingers fumbled, but he gripped it at last, a tiny roll of paper, frayed at the edge. He unrolled it slowly; held it out in front of him.

There were two words, written in pencil.

'*Help's coming.*'

Gratton read and re-read the note, his heart racing with excitement. If Dawlish said a thing was so, then it was so; incredible how he had come to look on Dawlish as a superman.

Better burn the note.

He read it again, although the two words were planted vividly in his mind, flicked his lighter, let the paper burn and then blew the tiny fragments of charred paper away.

He looked at his watch. It was nearly four o'clock. Clever beggar Fryer, to keep him on his own. But for that message from Dawlish, he would have been in the utter depths of depression. Now he felt quite light-hearted, although the first cold finger of doubt was entering his mind, the first question— how *could* Dawlish be so sure?

He began to examine the exhibits, reading the cards.

Roman crucible, circa A.D. 181—Merrance Caves.

Roman Flint, circa A.D. 95—Merrance Caves.

So all these things had been found in the locality. Nothing surprising in that.

The door began to open. Out of the tail of his eye Gratton saw Fryer enter, with Karloff behind him. Wild thoughts flashed through his mind. If he had smashed the glass he could have had a dozen weapons for the taking, but now it was too late.

Fryer said: 'Well, Gratton?'

Gratton did not speak.

'This time I am not acting,' Fryer said heavily. 'Unless you tell me what we want to know, you will be badly hurt. Where is Judy Bell?'

Gratton licked his lips.

'I don't know!'

'A fine story,' said Fryer impatiently. 'She was in the hotel with you, and I have the receptionist's word for it that she had lunch with you. She could not have disappeared completely in a few seconds.'

'It—it puzzles me as much as it does you,' muttered Gratton. He saw the knife in 'Karloff's' hand; and he hardly needed Fryer to tell him that he was serious. Another man, holding a gun, sidled into the room and approached Gratton. Karloff toyed with the knife and Fryer rolled a cigar from one side of his mouth to the other. His menace had never been greater. He had killed; and would kill again.

Fryer said: 'Gratton, you've been brought into this affair against your will. I don't want to hurt you *if* you're sensible. But I mean to know where Judy Bell is.'

The gunman stood close to Gratton's side.

Gratton said harshly: 'I tell you I don't know! She was—'

He broke off.

'Well, go on,' said Fryer in a reedy voice.

Something moved in the next room; a man shouted. Fryer

half-turned his head, Karloff looked round and the gunman's attention was distracted for a split second.

There would never be another opportunity like this!

Gratton rammed his elbow into the gunman's waist, and, as the man staggered away, the gun pointing to the ceiling, he jumped forward. Fryer saw him coming but before he could do anything Gratton drove his fist into the fat man's stomach. As Fryer fell backwards, he knocked against Karloff; Karloff jumped to one side, striking at Gratton with the knife.

It missed him.

Gratton kicked out at Karloff, and caught the man on the knee. It gave him time to spring into the next room and slam the door, although not enough to lock it.

He saw that Dawlish was in this room, and a gunman was with him. As Gratton hurtled through the doorway the gunman swung round. Gratton saw the gun pointing towards him, but at that second, Dawlish knocked the man's arm aside, and the bullet went wide. Dawlish followed this up with a vicious blow, and the gun flew from his hand.

The door of Gratton's room started to open.

'Down the stairs, Toby!' roared Dawlish. 'I'll hold 'em.'

Gratton obeyed him blindly. As he reached the main hall of the museum, a shot rang out. In a fury of excitement, Gratton reached the top of the stairs, gripped the handrail and vaulted over. It was a long drop to the passage below, but it was his only chance. Gratton was within a few yards of the main staircase now, running swiftly.

Pelting down the stairs he saw that the front door was closed. As he struggled with the fastening, the sounds of pursuit were perilously near. A shot rang out and a shower of falling plaster enveloped his head and shoulders; but the door was open.

Until then, he had not really thought he had a chance; but

now he was outside, *free*, and visibility was down to less than forty yards.

Three cars stood on the drive.

He paused for a split-second, wondering whether he dared take one of them; then he remembered the way the gates had been closed on him; that would happen again, if he were to get away it would have to be on foot. He turned left, away from the cliff; there would be no hope of escape that way again, but out on the hillside in the driving rain he might stand a chance.

He looked round.

Three men were running from the house towards him.

He sprinted towards the wall surrounding the house. Could he leap it? If he fumbled the jump it would be all up; better to spend a few seconds climbing and making sure that he could get over.

Wind blustered about him and he heard no sound of shooting. He was gasping for breath, and knew that he would soon have to rest.

He pulled up, then stretched his hands towards the wall, gripped the top lightly and hauled himself up. For three seconds he was a perfect target, and then, thankfully, he dropped to the other side.

He crouched down, water streaming from his hair, his face, getting into his eyes and his mouth.

The thicket would give him some cover.

He knew vaguely where it was, and turned and ran downhill. Here he was, *free*. The village was less than half a mile away; luck had been with him so far, he might get away with it.

There was the thicket!

He would be able to go more steadily now, and the fact that it was downhill would enable him to keep up a fair pace. He was sobbing for breath, but driven on by the relentless fact that this was the only chance for Dawlish and the others, the only chance of beating Fryer.

He felt hard ground beneath his feet. He was on the road!

Suddenly he saw the bridge. He could hear the river flowing beneath it. Two men were standing on the bridge. They must be Fryer's men. Who else would be standing, as guards, at the end of the bridge.

Suddenly they began to run.

Fifty yards from the bridge, they threw themselves flat on their stomachs. Gratton himself was less than twenty, still running at a fair speed, when he realised with horror that the bridge was about to be blown up.

CHAPTER TWENTY-TWO

DAWLISH KEEPS A PROMISE

He couldn't save himself now; he was too close to avoid the blast or flying debris if he flung himself down. All he could do was to try to put on an extra burst of speed.

He reached the end of the bridge, flogging his weary legs to make another effort. Had they mined both ends or just the end where they had been working when he had caught sight of them? If both ends—

The roar which came, deafened him, and the blast lifted him off his feet and flung him against the parapet. He hit the stone breastwork with a dull, body-shaking thud, and rolled over; but he had the sense to bury his head in his arms.

The bridge lurched under him.

He felt himself slipping and he realised at once that the bridge had been partly destroyed, and he was sliding down towards the river. He grabbed at the parapet and held on. His feet were hanging over the broken edge but—he was safe for the moment. After a pause, he crawled forward, frightened even to do that, for the bridge could be damaged in such a way that the slightest movement might send what was left of it crashing into the river.

He reached another pillar. Cautiously looking about him he saw that the bridge near Tor House had ceased to exist, but in front of him it was solid enough. He struggled to his hands and knees. The fall had hurt him more than he realised, but he forced himself to go on.

Funny thing, no one was about; they must have heard the explosion. Surely *someone* would come to see what was happening. And if he were to get a party together he would have to start quickly.

The full significance of what had happened to the bridge now dawned on him. *No one from Merrance could reach Tor House.* He had thought the bridge had been blown to stop him from getting away, but it had been planned before his escape, Fryer had made sure that he could not be taken unawares by an attack across the bridge.

Fryer had meant to cut himself off, to gain time, and—no one could now help the other prisoners at Tor House.

Gratton stood there in terrible indecision.

Why didn't someone come?

He looked towards Merrance—and men *were* coming, a little group of them. They were in uniform. *Police uniform!* And other policemen were getting out of a car which had pulled up at the end of Bridge Street.

Policemen—

Help had come.

Dawlish had kept his promise.

Two stalwart policemen carried Gratton between them, making a chair of their arms. Two policemen stood in the yard of the *Lobster Pot*, another in the entrance. He stood aside as Gratton was carried into the hall and then up the stairs. He was taken to his own room and lowered to a chair. A tall, good-looking, man in plainclothes held a glass of brandy to his lips.

God! it did him good. He said unsteadily:

'Who are you?'

'Superintendent Trivett of New Scotland Yard,' the man said, adding with a grim smile: 'I'm by way of being a friend of Patrick Dawlish's, and had an urgent message from him this morning. Can you tell me what it's all about?'

Gratton said slowly:

'I don't know. I don't think even Dawlish does. But I can tell you this . . .'

Trivett made no comment, but his lips settled into a long tight line as he listened. Gratton sketched what had led up to their journey to Merrance and passed quickly over what had happened that morning. He would have preferred to say nothing about the earlier events, but this man impressed him as being determined to know as much as he could. As he talked, the urgency of the situation grew on him, and he finished sharply:

'And the quicker you're at Tor House the better. I don't know whether there's a chance to save Dawlish and the others. If there is, it's a pretty slim one.'

'I shouldn't worry too much,' said Trivett reassuringly. 'Another party has gone to Tor house—they started off immediately after the bridge was blown, by jeep. Fryer forgot jeeps,' he added with another grim smile. 'The men are at the house by now and I'm going to join them as soon as I've word—we're in touch by walkie-talkie radio,' he added. His offhand manner reminded Gratton vividly of Dawlish. 'Everything we can do is being done, but—I can't get to the bottom of it, Mr. Gratton. You say that you withheld information about this from the police at Dawlish's request.'

'Well—'

'I know,' said Trivett, 'you don't want to let Dawlish down. But surely you didn't agree without making a protest, there must have been some satisfying reason why you kept away from us. Fear?' he added abruptly.

Gratton said: 'I don't think I was particularly afraid. I didn't like it, but—no, Dawlish convinced me it was wise, and I think Judy Bell convinced him.'

'I see. And this girl disappeared from a room along here.'

'Yes. How it was done is beyond me,' confessed Gratton. 'I wasn't out of the room more than three minutes.'

'Hmm,' said Trivett. 'I'll see what I can find out. You'd better have your second hot bath and get into some dry clothes.'

Dry clothes were a problem; but Gratton did not waste much time worrying about them. If necessary, he could borrow something. He soaked in a hot bath, so tired after his race to the village that the sense of urgency had quite gone. Trivett and his men would look after things now. For all he knew, the affair might be over as far as he was concerned. Slowly, resentment at that possibility crept over him. While there was a chance to help Dawlish, he wanted to take it.

He rubbed himself down vigorously, put on a dressing-gown and went across to his room.

He turned to the door—and it opened, to admit the receptionist who asked apologetically, if Gratton could spare him a moment.

'Yes, of course,' said Gratton, 'and then you can borrow a change of clothes for me.'

'I'm sure we shall be able to manage that, sir,' said the receptionist earnestly, 'but there's another little matter—'

Gratton asked him what it was and the old man came nearer, his voice sinking to a conspiratorial whisper. It appeared that he knew where Judy was, and at that Gratton could have shaken him with impatience.

'Where? Where?'

'In the caves.' It seemed that they ran under the inn, and could be reached by a sliding panel in the upstair room.

It was characteristic of Trivett. Gratton thought, that he did not reprimand the receptionist for withholding the information from him, but simply asked to be taken down to the cellars. By then, Gratton had borrowed a wearable tweed suit and a pair of thick brown shoes. He went downstairs with Trivett, a constable and the receptionist, who led the way down a narrow flight of stone steps to the cellar. Gratton wondered if, even now, they might be walking into a trap.

A man called from the top of the stairs.

'Superintendent! Are you there?'

'Yes,' said Trivett, turning round. 'What is it?'

'News from the house, sir. We've taken possession.'

Gratton caught his breath.

'The house is empty except for two dead men and an old woman who's nearly demented, sir. One of the men is Sir Henry Reddelow, and the other hasn't yet been identified.'

Gratton exclaimed: 'Freddie!' He grew aware of Trivett staring at him intently.

'Both of them had been shot at close quarters. One other matter of consequence, sir, is that there was an explosion in the cellars immediately after our men's arrival.'

'Check everything,' ordered Trivett, 'and I'll be up in ten minutes or so.'

The receptionist started on again, weaving between great bins half-filled with bottles, which were covered with dust and cobwebs.

Gratton was glad that the two policemen had followed. They stood in the narrow cellar, with the ceiling almost touching their heads. Gratton thought again that this might be a trap, and Fryer, not Dawlish, may have bribed the receptionist.

'Bit creepy down here,' said Trivett.

Gratton grunted.

If the lights were to go out . . .

With the help of Trivett's two men, a dozen great barrels were shifted; and behind them was a heavy-looking wooden door, studded with iron nails. On a hook in the ceiling hung a heavy key. The little old man took it down and pushed it into the lock.

The lock clicked back.

'Now we won't be long,' he said, and pulled.

The door wouldn't move.

He tried again, and then stood back, gaping at the door.

'It—it's fastened on the *inside*,' he gasped, 'the young lady must have locked herself in. But how could she have done that? There are bolts, they haven't been used for countless years, the last time I saw them they were quite immovable.'

Gratton said harshly: 'We must get in there, we can't fail her now. Fryer's probably been here, he may have—'

'Steady,' said Trivett. 'Let's have the door down.'

CHAPTER TWENTY-THREE

DARK SECRET

The worst part of it all was not knowing what had happened; and what might follow.

When the door was broken down, the rusty bolts were examined; only someone with exceptional strength could have shot them home. The receptionist talked nervously. He swore that he had locked the door from force of habit—it had been an unwritten rule of the *Lobster Pot* that the door of the tunnel should be kept locked.

According to his story, Dawlish had asked him if there was a safe hiding place, and he had told him of the tunnel. And the girl had insisted on going right inside and not staying in the cellars.

Trivett and his men used powerful torches to examine the stony floor of the tunnel; they found several traces of the recent passing to and fro of a number of men. As they worked, the receptionist talked more freely. There was no map of the caves and the tunnels as far as he knew, but rumour had it that the caves linked Cliff Tor to River Caves.

Gratton felt sure that this was true.

Judy had come to hide here, thinking herself safe; and Fryer's men, knowing that there was another entrance to the caves through this tunnel, had come along, blocked it up—and undoubtedly, seen and caught her.

'How large are these caves?' asked Trivett.

'Enormous, sir,' said the receptionist, 'the cliffs are very dangerous because of them. The men will have to stay here until the gale blows itself out. If the weather were calm then they could have made off by boat, but I don't think any ship could live in these seas so near the shore. There's only one way they could go, if as you say your men are in possession of Tor House and the jetty there. They would have to come right through the caves to the River Caves themselves and take off from the base of the cliffs.'

'So we can get 'em,' said Trivett softly. 'If we send a party through the caves and another over the hill to guard the cliffs, they can't get away.'

Gratton said: 'No, but—'

'Go on,' said Trivett.

'They'll probably try to strike a bargain; their safety for Dawlish's and—Miss Bell's.'

'We'll see about that,' said Trivett. 'You're coming along, I suppose?'

'I am,' said Gratton grimly. 'But don't imagine that it's going to be easy. Fryer will post guards all along the route. In any case, they'll probably blow them up.'

'Oh, no!' cried the receptionist. 'I don't think they dare do that. If there should be an explosion in any part of the caves the result would be disastrous. The whole cliff would collapse into the sea. The whole *cliff*, gentlemen!'

Gratton, with Trivett by his side, was leading the party through the caves. They had reached the main natural formations ten minutes before, and were making their way slowly towards the river caves. Three of them had dim torches; and Trivett held a fourth, which spread only a faint light a few feet in front of them.

In Gratton's mind was the receptionist's warning, and the last fatalistic words: '*The whole cliff, gentlemen.*' Fryer must know of it; surely Fryer wouldn't risk being buried alive?

There was no telling what the man would do.

Suddenly, something moved ahead of them.

A stone rolled, a sharp intake of breath from someone not far away from them—someone *above* them. Gratton looked up sharply, and Trivett raised the torch. It shone on a woman's shoes! A woman was crouching on a ledge in the cave. Gratton could hardly hear himself speak because of the thumping of his heart.

'Judy—is that you?'

A tense silence; then: '*Toby!*'

The girl dropped to the floor of the cave. She approached them quickly—urgently. And suddenly Gratton moved forward and hugged her, pressing her so tightly to him that she gasped for breath.

'What are you doing here?' demanded Trivett.

'Keep your voice low,' urged Judy. 'I was in the caves when several of Fryer's men came along the tunnel. I hid in a recess, and saw them bolt the door; when they went back, I followed them. They joined Fryer and—and the others a little further along. They're still there.'

'*All* the others?' asked Trivett softly.

'I don't know, but I caught a glimpse of Jeremy and Beresford,' said Judy.

'I wonder how many men Fryer has with him,' mused Trivett.

'Seven or eight at least,' Judy said. Her face looked pale and strained in the dim light, and she still clutched Gratton's arm. 'The awful thing is—'

She broke off.

'Yes?' said Trivett.

She said: 'There are fifty or sixty people in these caves. Fryer's kept them here for weeks. I don't know who they are, or anything about them, only that he's brought them here one by one. He threatened me that if ever I sent for the police or asked for help he'd kill them all. It was because of that I tried to make Dawlish give up. Even now—'

Again she broke off; the horror of the fifty or sixty human beings with death hovering over their heads filled them all. Gratton understood why she had behaved so strangely.

No wonder Fryer had felt himself safe, had believed that in the final struggle between himself and Dawlish, he would—by threatening to destroy these captivated people—hold the trump card.

No one spoke for a long time. Gratton, with Judy's fingers tight about his arm, stared into the gloom and tried to think. So much was plain now, but—was there a solution, was there a way of making Fryer give up?

Trivett asked softly:

'How far away are they?'

'Not very far,' said Judy, 'there were two men on guard about fifty yards along . . .'

Silence fell upon the group of waiting men; and through it came a little sound, which grew louder. Someone was walking towards them, without making any attempt to hide his approach. Trivett put his torch on the ledge where Judy had been hiding, and backed away; whoever was coming would be visible in the light of the torch, but would not be able to see them.

The footsteps drew louder; nearer.

Claude came into sight!

He walked slowly, his eyes narrowed against the light; his shoulders drooped, and his face was set in lines of hopelessness, as if he had seen a vision of great horror and could not shut the sight out of his mind.

Claude said: 'So you've come, Bill?' There was no liveliness in his voice, for the first time Gratton heard him speak without a trace of his usual high spirits. 'Fryer's sent me with a message,' Claude continued. 'He wants Judy. And he wants the cave emptied and the men removed from the top of the cliff.'

'I dare say he does,' said Trivett, drily.

Claude said: 'And he's likely to get it. Ultimatum, Bill. If the men aren't withdrawn and if he doesn't get Judy in the next hour, he'll blow the caves in. Argument being that if you catch him he'll have to die anyway, so he may as well do as much damage as possible before he goes. Bargaining weapons: Ted, Tim, a man named Grey, and fifty-odd human beings packed in one of the caves near the edge of the cliff. I've seen the T.N.T. and I know he means business.'

He looked straight at Judy.

'You can't go,' said Gratton hoarsely.

Silence fell; and with every passing second the full fiendishness of Fryer's final ultimatum struck home. Gratton thought dully that it wasn't only those fifty 'unknowns'—but wait a moment! Claude hadn't mentioned Dawlish!

'Where's Pat!' he demanded sharply.

'Don't know,' Claude said. 'He escaped from Tor House. Thought he was with you. But even Pat couldn't find a way out of this one. Fryer says—don't know how true it is—that if he explodes the T.N.T. then the cliff will fall into the sea. He seems to have it all worked out.'

Judy clutched Gratton's arm again. 'Perhaps there *is* something I can do.'

'There's nothing.' Gratton said roughly.

'What do you mean?' asked Trivett.

'I can go to Fryer,' said Judy slowly, 'and I might be able to—to prevent him from touching off the T.N.T. I don't know how, but there might be a chance. I've got to *try*,' she exclaimed fiercely. 'Toby, I've got to try, it's no use looking at me like that!'

Gratton said: 'Try if you must, but if you do, I'm coming with you.'

CHAPTER TWENTY-FOUR

T.N.T.

The guard at the entrance to the next cave made them put up their hands, and patted their clothes to make sure that neither of them carried a gun; then he allowed them to pass. They went through the same performance at the second cave.

In the third, Fryer and several of his men waited; and in a group apart, with an armed guard standing over them, were Dawlish's friends and 'Grey'. No one spoke as Gratton and Judy entered. Fryer continued to smoke. If he were satisfied to see Judy, he showed no sign, but waited until she drew near; then he stretched out a hand and took her wrist.

'Is Trivett taking his men away?'

'He wants to talk to you,' said Judy. That was what she had arranged with Trivett to say. 'He won't leave the caves until he's spoken to you.'

'Oh, won't he?' asked Fryer.

He shot a glance towards Karloff, who stood by the entrance to another cavern. Gratton stared at the ugly man and beyond him. He saw that a hole had been drilled in the rock wall and a thin flex inserted, leading to a hole at Karloff's feet.

'Oh, won't he?' repeated Fryer. 'Gratton, listen to me. You're to go back to the police. You're to tell them that if he hasn't cleared out of the cave inside an hour, I shall blow it open. I'm not fooling. I know the stakes. If he gets me, I'm finished—so are my men. We'd rather go out this way than be caught. If he'll clear the caves and the cliffs and wait until the storm blows itself out, I'll leave everyone here alive. *Everyone.*' he added, and suddenly leaping up he pushed back a piece of wood hanging on the wall, disclosing a hole rather larger than a man's hand.

'*Look,*' he said.

Gratton saw faces, thin, emaciated, with pale, glittering eyes, packed tightly in a small cavern.

From the hole came a foul stench which made Gratton's stomach heave.

Judy said passionately: 'Why make *them* suffer!'

'You recognise them then?' queried Fryer. 'Your displaced persons—the people you wanted to help! The hounded, the persecuted. All those of them who had money and could pay for their passage, that is. You little, naive fool! I got them into England under the cover of your famous rest camps, and Reddelow fixed their permits—he didn't know what he was doing at first. If you hadn't sent for Dawlish I'd have got them out of the country one by one. All they want is to leave Europe, and they'll pay a fortune to do it. There's a million pounds in that cave—a million poundsworth of stinking men and women! I made Reddelow help, I made Appleyard help, I blackmailed them all into it, all of them! And I've been doing this for years! I've shipped hundreds across the Atlantic and I'd have shipped plenty more if Dawlish—'

He caught his breath, hardly able to get the last words out. Now he stood glaring at Judy, stretching out his hand towards her.

'But you'll pay for it, Judy, if they let me get away from here you'll pay for it, and if they don't you'll be blown up with the rest of us. Gratton, go back and tell Trivett and Dawlish. Hurry! An hour—that's all the time you've got, an hour—sixty minutes— just sixty minutes. Get out. Gratton! Get out!'

His voice rose to a scream.

'*Get out!*' screamed Fryer, and struck him across the face.

Gratton turned and staggered towards the exit; he could do nothing. No one could help, and Trivett would have to make that awful decision. Yet he was only a few yards from the T.N.T. If he turned round, if he ignored the gun in Karloff's hand, he might reach the fuse, in the confusion Beresford and Jeremy might be able to help.

He glanced over his shoulder, to see Karloff covering him with his revolver, and others, at the sides of the cavern, pointing guns towards him. He kicked against a stone, and stumbled. Perhaps that was why the boulder behind Karloff appeared to move. He steadied, glanced round again—

It was gathering momentum, swaying from the top, only a few inches from Karloff's head. Suddenly the great stone lurched forward, falling across Karloff's legs. He screamed, and his gun hit the rocky floor and slithered across to Gratton's feet.

Gratton snatched it up. A shot rang out and a bullet hummed over his head. He fired at one of the gunmen; the second was falling from a terrific blow from Beresford. Jeremy darted forward and whipped the gun from the falling man's hand. One of the guards rushed towards the boulder, but Gratton, seeing everything with vivid clarity, realised that the boulder had covered the fuse. Karloff, crushed and helpless, now moaned and waved his hands; Beresford and Jeremy were holding back the men who stood by the walls, Gratton covered Fryer.

Suddenly Dawlish was there, though no one saw him come, or how he came.

And Trivett and his men came running.

'Well,' said Dawlish, cheerfully. 'When Toby made the dash from the house I followed him and went to earth—I'd seen a man coming out of the ground, as it were, and guessed he came from the caves. I'd a suspicion of the truth, and lost no time searching until I found the crowd. Then Fryer's men appeared on the scene, and I slipped into the inner cave. None of the poor beggars gave me away. I heard what was planned, and judged that the hole for T.N.T. was being drilled in the rock near the entrance, and I thought the one chance was to push the boulder away—it had been put into position to keep us locked in. It took me ten minutes to shift the thing, I started when you and Judy arrived, and I thought I'd have to give it up! Persistence pays, you see.' He looked at Trivett. 'Doesn't it, Bill?'

Trivett said soberly: 'Sometimes.'

They were back in the *Lobster Pot*. The whole party was there, Gratton and Judy sitting together on a sofa, Beresford, Jeremy, and Claude squatting on the floor.

In every man's hand was a tankard of local brew.

'Be generous, old chap,' said Dawlish pleadingly. 'If ever there was a case for using my own judgment, this was it. First Paul, then Judy, made me feel sure that something pretty foul would happen if the police were brought in too early. Directly I knew that we couldn't finish the job ourselves, I sent you that S.O.S. through Claude. I don't think you've a very strong case for complaint, you know.'

'The Assistant Commissioner and the Home Office might,' said Trivett.

'Think again, Bill! Reddelow dished out entrance permits to men who should never have come into the country. We now know that he was blackmailed into doing it. The truth leaked out, he was asked to "resign" and all was hush-hush—to avoid scandal. It will be hush-hush again, believe me! Immediately I knew Reddelow was mixed up in it I had an idea of the truth. The d.p's had either been smuggled out of the country or were held somewhere until they could be sent abroad—and the caves seemed as good a concentration camp as any. Taken by and large, Bill, I don't think I'll get even a rap over the knuckles. After all, would they have lived if you'd been advised?'

Trivett made no comment, but sipped his beer.

'We now know how it was all planned,' said Dawlish. 'Fryer won't open his mouth but Karloff has told us plenty. Freddie—Reddelow—Paul—Judy—all blackmailed or otherwise persuaded to help. Fryer was the leader, although he tried to deny it. The rest centre scheme used as a facade to cover the movement of D.P's, most of them being political refugees with assets abroad, men who couldn't get out legally because they couldn't get visas. I don't know what Freddie's black secret was, but he's paid hard for whatever he did.'

Trivett said: 'We'll leave it like that for the time being. Meanwhile, I want you to come up to Tor House and identify Reddelow.' He looked at Gratton and Judy as he spoke, for he had heard the whole story. 'It won't take long,' he said.

'All right,' agreed Gratton.

Before they left the room, however, the door opened and the receptionist looked in.

'A trunk call, Mr. Dawlish, sir, Mrs. Dawlish—'

Dawlish was on his feet in a flash; and when Gratton and the others passed the telephone kiosk, they heard him bellow:

'Thank God you're all right . . . Yes, yes, the show's over . . .'

*   *   *

At Tor House, Gratton and Judy looked down at the haggard face of Sir Henry Reddelow. Judy did not hesitate to speak:

'That's the man I saw at the tennis club,' she said quietly, and Trivett looked questioningly at Gratton.

'Know him?' he asked.

Gratton said heavily: 'Oh, yes. We knew him as Speck. Sour old beggar.'

'I see,' said Trivett. 'We knew that Reddelow had another identity, but we didn't know what. He used to own that house near Harrow, and had a special building for his museum, but he came back here years ago.'

He drew the sheet over the dead man's face.

A warm September sun bathed the courts of the *Sola Club*. On Number 1 Court, young Plomley was playing a neck to neck game with a new member. On another court Dawlish and Felicity, Tim Jeremy and his wife, were playing a foursome. Claude sat in a deck chair, with a handkerchief over his eyes. Only Beresford and 'Grey'—who was now the owner of Tor House—were missing from the party which had been in the caves, for on the verandah of the club-house Gratton and Judy stood watching.

'Well,' Gratton said gruffly, 'there it is, Judy. I'm worth about sixpence and you—anyhow, I love you. I think I loved you from the first moment I set eyes on you, but—for the love of Mike tell me I haven't a chance and be done with it!'

Judy turned and looked at him.

'Judy!' cried Gratton.

Claude exposed one benevolent eye from under the handkerchief, and quickly covered it again.

ABOUT THE AUTHOR

John Creasey, born in 1908, was a paramount English crime and science fiction writer who used myriad pseudonyms for more than six hundred novels. He founded the UK Crime Writers' Association in 1953. In 1962, his book *Gideon's Fire* received the Edgar Award for Best Novel from the Mystery Writers of America. Many of the characters featured in Creasey's titles became popular, including George Gideon of Scotland Yard, who was the basis for a subsequent television series and film. Creasey died in Salisbury, UK, in 1973.

THE PATRICK DAWLISH MYSTERIES

FROM OPEN ROAD MEDIA

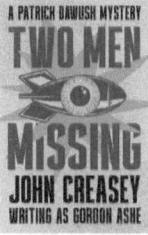

OPEN ROAD

INTEGRATED MEDIA

OPEN ROAD
INTEGRATED MEDIA

Find a full list of our authors and
titles at www.openroadmedia.com

FOLLOW US
@OpenRoadMedia